tek
money

tek money

WILLIAM SHATNER

AN ACE/PUTNAM BOOK · PUBLISHED BY G.P. PUTNAM'S SONS NEW YORK

G. P. PUTNAM'S SONS
Publishers Since 1838
200 Madison Avenue
New York, NY 10016

Library of Congress Cataloging-in-Publication Data

Shatner, William.
Tek money / William Shatner.
p.   cm.
ISBN 0-399-14109-X
"The seventh book in a futuristic thriller series featuring
Detective Jake Cardigan."
1. Cardigan, Jake (Fictitious character)—Fiction.   2. Private
investigators—Fiction.   I. Title.
PS3569.H347T444   1995   95-8686 CIP
813'.54—dc20

Book Design by Julie Duquet

Printed in the United States of America
1   3   5   7   9   10   8   6   4   2
This book is printed on acid-free paper. ∞

(1.00)

Toiling in his toilet and sometimes at his desk, Ron Goulart has written his little heart out. His work on these novels has been unheralded for the most part, and I would like to blow a trumpet for him right now. Hail to Ron Goulart, noblest scribe of the Tek World.

ACKNOWLEDGMENTS

*Deserving less than a trumpet but more than a flute
are the hard-working:*

Carmen LaVia
Susan Allison
Ivy Fischer Stone

Perhaps a roll of drums for all.

tek
money

1

Peter Traynor was having trouble getting to where he wanted to go.

It was a hot, dry, restless night in late October of the year 2121. A raw, feverish wind was knifing across the night beach in the Malibu Sector of Greater Los Angeles, rattling the long twisty row of decorative palm trees, snatching at Traynor's sleeve, shoving him off balance.

His difficulties had grown worse ever since he set his skycar down at the seaside lot and started making his way along the dark sand. It was probably because of that damned stopover in the Venice Sector. He'd promised himself he was through with that sort of thing.

A lean, lighthaired man of forty one, Traynor stumbled as a sharp new gust of hot wind hit at him. He fell to his knees on the harsh sand, putting out both palms to save himself from toppling over completely.

"Jesus!"

One of his hands had touched the face of a dead man who was partially buried in the gritty sand. Thick blood was smeared all across the dead face, great splashes of it. As he struggled to pull away clear, Traynor managed to drag the corpse with him. He struggled, but couldn't seem to disentangle himself.

"Don't you recognize me, Pete?" asked the dead man, smiling with his bloody lips. "It's me—Flanders."

"You're five weeks dead, Flanders," he shouted at him. "I had nothing to do with it."

Crying out, Traynor rolled to his left, kicking out, crawling away from the smiling corpse.

The harsh sand slowed his progress, scraping at his clothes. The wind grew even hotter as it came swirling around him.

"What's wrong, dear?"

He hadn't noticed until now that his wife—well, actually, his former wife since November of 2120—was standing only a few feet away. Slim and pretty in a long white dress, wearing one of her black ribbons to hold back her russet hair.

"I came here to . . ." He paused, shaking his head the way you do when you're trying to come fully awake. "I have to see Jake Cardigan. He lives along here someplace, but I'm having a bad reaction to—"

"Not a very good idea, is that, Peter?" suggested his ex-wife. "You don't want, really, to talk to anyone right now, least of all a private investigator."

"I didn't quite catch what you said, Amy." He took a few shaky steps in her direction, glancing down to make sure he wasn't going to step on the corpse.

But the dead man had moved. He was sitting, cross-legged, over on a white neo-iron bench. He had his shirt pulled open wide and was probing a gaping lazgun wound in his chest with two bloody fingers.

"Leave me the hell alone, Flanders," he yelled. "I didn't know what was going to happen."

When Traynor looked again toward his wife, he was just in time to see her catch fire and begin to burn. She was soon completely surrounded by a crackling roar of bright orange flame.

"Amy!"

"As I was saying, Peter, you're not being at all smart," she resumed. "Go home now and forget this nonsense. You don't, not at all, need a detective."

He pressed all the fingers of his right hand to his temple. "There's something I've found out—I told you a little bit about it, Amy, the last time I came to see the kids. It's worse than I thought and I've got to do something."

"No, that isn't necessary at all." The flames were taking her over, sending a high flickering torch of fire up into the dark windy night. "You're only upset because you and Dennis had a disagreement."

"I can't argue now—I'm not thinking very straight." He moved, unsteadily, closer to her. The flames that were consuming her gave off no heat. "Don't get mad and criticize me—I know I shouldn't have stopped at that Tek parlor."

Amy disintegrated, turning to dark, leafy ashes and drifting away on the wind.

Traynor clenched his fists, pressed them, hard, into his ribs. Would have been a hell of a lot better to have come straight here, instead of stopping for that damned Tek session. Sometimes, though, he felt a lot better, a lot braver, afterward. But tonight, something was wrong. He was having painful flashbacks, unwanted illusions, and they seemed to be getting worse.

After a moment, struggling hard, he was able to regain control of himself again. Things were okay once more and he was sure he could hold off any further hallucinations.

Traynor could remember Jake Cardigan's address now. He knew exactly where to find the beachside condo. He remembered, too, everything he had to talk over with him.

"Jake's just about the only person in Greater LA that I can trust."

Six big black candles were burning up ahead on the beach, each in a man-high golden holder. They circled a plain coffin that was resting on a metal rack.

He halted, gripping one hand tightly in the other, fighting what was happening to him. "Nothing is really there," he reminded himself. "Nothing at all. This is just another damned Tek fantasy."

The coffin didn't go away.

He'd long since recognized it. He remembered it from

twenty one years ago. A closed coffin, because of the way his mother had died.

Now, slowly and silently, the coffin lid began to rise.

Traynor put his hands up over his eyes, but he discovered he could see right through them.

His mother's charred and blackened body sat up and shook its head. "You shouldn't be out so late, dear," she cautioned. "Best go right home now, darling. You don't really want to visit this detective."

"I have to, Mom. I've found out something—stumbled on it. A lot of bad things are going to happen unless—"

"You're Pete Traynor, aren't you? Is something wrong?"

About thirty feet up beyond his mother's coffin a lean teenage young man was standing, watching him.

"I'm looking for Jake Cardigan," he managed to say. "You're his son?"

"That's right, yes," answered Dan. "You don't look so well. Is there—"

"I've got to talk to him right away."

"Dad's not at home, but he should be soon. Come on over on the deck and sit down, Mr. Traynor."

The only way to get over to Dan Cardigan and the condo building that rose up behind him was by walking through the coffin.

"Don't keep on with this, son," warned his mother.

Traynor said to Dan Cardigan, "I know about the hijacking of—"

That was all he got to say.

A huge roaring began in his ears. He heard cries of

pain and the boom of thunder and dark, discordant music.

His mother tried to embrace him. "Poor Pete, poor baby."

Before she touched him, his brain seemed to explode inside his skull and he felt his life go spinning away on the red wind.

THE BEARDED MAN was saying, "Our revels now are ended. These our actors, as I foretold you, were all spirits and are . . ."

The strap on Jake Cardigan's wristwatch phone began to contract and expand against his flesh. A handsome, somewhat weatherbeaten man of almost fifty, he leaned forward in his amphitheater seat and held the small instrument close to his right ear before activating the speaker button.

Dan's voice said anxiously, "Dad, you'd better get home. There's been a death and—"

His son's voice was suddenly cut off.

Frowning, Jake tapped out his home number on the wristphone.

The pretty blonde woman in the next seat spoke a question close to his ear. "Something wrong?"

"Not sure, Bev," he answered in a whisper. "Dan called, then got cut off."

The phone at home rang again and again. Dan didn't answer.

Jake said to Bev Kendricks, "Sounds like Dan may be in trouble." After pointing a thumb at the nearest exit to the Beverly Hills Sector Shakespeare HoloTheatre, he eased up to his feet and started making his way along the dark row of seats.

Bev rose up and followed him. "Excuse me."

Down on the circular stage the hologram actors continued with *The Tempest*.

2

The skycar bounced slightly as Jake guided it through the windy night. He tapped into the homesec system at the condo he shared with his son, and asked it, "Give me a report on what's going on."

"Everything is normal, sir," came a tinny voice out of the small voxbox in the dash panel.

"Pictures, room by room," requested Jake as the skycar carried them toward his home.

"I'm sure he's okay," said Bev, who was sitting, leaning forward, in the passenger seat beside him.

"Yeah, probably," he conceded, watching the monitor screen as it took him on a tour of the apartment. "It's just that—well, people that I'm fond of have a tendency to get hurt."

"That's nonsense. Beth Kittridge was killed by the Teklords to keep her from testifying, Jake," the blonde detective assured him. "It had not a damned thing to do with you."

"I could've stopped it, if I hadn't let them sidetrack me."

She put a hand on his. "Been quite a while since that happened. You've got to work harder at forgetting it."

"No sign of any trouble anywhere," he said, watching the screen. "But, damn it, no sign of Dan either."

"We'll be there in a few more minutes. Relax, talk about the play."

"I like real actors better than holos," said Jake. "And I thought the guy playing Caliban was too cute to—what the hell is this?"

The skycar was gliding down toward the landing area next to the condo building. There was a lot of extra illumination down there and it showed two large, squat SoCal Police skyvans sitting at the lot edge. There were at least a dozen uniformed cops and a couple of scene-of-the-crime robots scattered across the beach that fronted the building. And sprawled at the water's edge, where the surf was licking at it, was a spread-eagled body.

"Is that Dan?" Jake leaned close to the sidewindow, scowling down into the approaching glare.

"Too tall, not enough hair," said Bev. "Take it easy."

As the sky car started to settle down for a landing in its usual spot, a grating beep noise started coming out of one of the dash voxboxes. "Police emergency," announced a deep, rough voice. "Police emergency. No landings allowed in this area."

"I live here!" Jake took over the landing manually and set the craft down, ignoring the beep and the repeated warnings.

A thickset uniformed officer came running to the car door as Jake opened it and stepped out. "Where the hell," said Jake, "is my son and—"

"Hands up over your head, mister, quick!" ordered the cop, leveling a stungun at Jake. "Suppose you tell me why you disregarded an official warning and landed—"

"Rudy?" Bev got, very carefully, out on her side. "It's me, Bev Kendrick."

The cop glanced over at her, lowering his gun a few inches. "What's a legit private eye like you doing here?"

"This is Jake Cardigan's place and I happen to be with him tonight." She walked around the front of the maroon skycar.

"Cardigan? I've heard of him—excon, onetime Tek-runner."

Jake took a few steps closer to the man. "Where's my son?"

"You don't understand the procedure, Cardigan," said Rudy, the gunbarrel swinging up again. "Maybe too much Tek has cooked your goddamn brains. We ask the questions, friend, and you answer them. Right now we've got a dead man just about in your front yard. So suppose—"

"Rudy, ease off," advised Bev, touching his arm with a

warning tap. "I really don't think you want to annoy Jake just now."

Looking away from the angry officer, Jake spotted Dan now. A lean black cop was holding on to the front of Dan's shirt, shaking him. They were down at the edge of the night sea.

Jake gave a quick shake of his head, turned away from Rudy and started down across the dark sand. "Get your damn hands off him, Drexler," he called.

Detective Lieutenant Len Drexler turned and glowered in Jake's direction. He made a low snorting noise and let go of the young man. "We have what looks like a Tek killing here, Cardigan," he said evenly. "Your kid is pretty certainly involved in—"

"Dan's not involved in a damn thing." Jake grabbed hold of the front of the detective's jacket. "And even if he is, you'd better not rough him up. Now, without any further bullshit, tell me exactly what's going on."

Drexler jerked back, freeing himself from Jake's grasp. "You're excited," he decided, "so I'll excuse your man-handling me, Cardigan." He moved nearer to the corpse. "This guy's a Tekhead, a heavy user—and it's my guess somebody slipped him a sizzler. You probably know what that is, since you used to work in the Tek trade. A sizzler is one of those special Tek chips thought up by your Teklord cronies to take care of users they want to get rid of. Initially it acts like your ordinary chip, giving the bastard whatever fantasies he orders up on his damn Brainbox." Frowning, the officer kicked the dead man in the side. "Later on, though, usually in a matter of hours, the victim's brain starts to short out and crash. Before that there are all sorts of uncontrollable hallucinations. Witnesses say they heard this guy yelling and howling all along this stretch of beach while on his way to pay you a social call." He kicked at the body again. "Jesus, you can practically smell the fried brains."

Jake put an arm around his son's shoulders. "You okay?"

"Sure, sorry about the phone. These cops got here while I was in the middle of my call to you," explained Dan. "Wouldn't let me finish or answer when you tried to phone back."

"You know anything about him?"

"It's Peter Traynor," answered Dan. "He tried to see you a couple of times about a year or so ago. I recognized him when I came out to see what the noise was about."

"Traynor?" Jake's brow wrinkled as he knelt beside the dead man. The lean face was twisted in agony even now. "Yeah, it's Traynor sure enough. Looks like he went further down the chutes since I saw him last."

"Isn't Peter Traynor an old Tekkie buddy of yours, Cardigan?" Drexler squatted in the damp sand beside Jake. "What was he coming to see you about? Picking up a new supply of Tek chips maybe?"

Jake, slowly, rose to his feet, pulling the black cop up with him by the collar. "Let's establish something for good and all, Drexler," he said. "I don't use Tek and haven't for years. And, as you and all your gang know damn well, I was never a dealer. That whole charge was a frame and it's been cleaned off my record. If you're trying to pass yourself off as even a halfway competent cop, you ought to keep up with what's going on."

"C'mon, Cardigan, everybody knows that Bascom bribed the right people to get your record fancied up," Drexler told him, laughing. "The Cosmos Detective Agency is powerful enough in Greater LA to do things like that. Now, if I had a little more influence myself, I'd do an investigation of Walt Bascom and some of his trickier operatives. Notably you and that greaser partner of yours, Sid Gomez."

"No, Jake." Bev caught hold of his arm and yanked him back just as Jake was about to swing on the lieutenant.

Drexler took a few steps back. "Sorry I called your partner names, Cardigan," he said in a murmuring voice. "Now, what can you tell me about Traynor and why he was coming to call on you?"

"I met Traynor for the first time years ago, before I went to prison," said Jake. "Yeah, and I did run into the guy in some of the Tek parlors that we were both frequenting. I saw him again about a year or more ago, when he came by to ask me to help him out with some trouble he was having with his ex-wife." Jake shook his head. "I knew the guy was still on Tek and I didn't want to get involved with him or his problems. I gave him the name of a divorce attorney in the Glendale Sector. As I recall, he came back a few times more to try to see me when I wasn't here."

"Twice." Dan held up two fingers.

"Tell me about tonight," urged the police detective. "Why was he coming here? What'd he want?"

"That I don't know." He let his right hand drop to his side and Bev took hold of it. "He didn't vidphone in advance, if that's what you're asking. I had no idea he was going to show up."

Drexler pointed at Dan. "Maybe the kid knows."

"He didn't call here at all," said Dan. "And we sure didn't have much in the way of a conversation when he did show up. I heard him out here, he was shouting and I thought he was with someone." He shook his head. "When I came out, he was alone and he looked very upset and disheveled. I figured he'd fallen in the sand a few times. I said a few words to him and—well, that was when he died. I thought he had some kind of seizure."

"Yeah, a rigged seizure." Drexler's frown deepened and he scratched at his ribs. "We'll drop the questions for now, Cardigan, even though I got a feeling you do know what Traynor was up to tonight."

"Just so your feelings don't inspire you to bother my son again."

"I got a robot forensic team due any minute," the lieutenant told them. "Why don't you and Bev and the kid take a hike along the beach? Stay away a couple hours. I'd truly appreciate that."

Jake said, "Okay, we'll keep off. But remember that Traynor never got inside my place. I don't want you or your goons in there either."

"Got something to hide?"

Before Jake could reply, Bev tugged him out of range of the policeman. "Let's take that walk," she advised. "Come on along, Dan."

3

The copperplated robot waitress at the AllNite Neptune Cafe had been in service there for close to seven years and hadn't gone in for a tune-up in nearly two. She was as amiable as ever, but sometimes moved with a slight wobble and now and then you could hear her inner workings whirring and sputtering. When Gomez, his dark curly hair and moustache dotted with night mist, came strolling into the long, narrow seaside restaurant, she straightened up, making a chuckling noise, and went lurching up to him. "Hiya, stranger," she said. "Long time no see."

The detective smiled and returned her hug. *"Buenas noches,* my love," he said. "I'm hunting for my *amigos*—did they drop in here?"

"If you mean Sourpuss," she said, nodding her coppery head in the direction of the rear of the place, "he's back there with his son and a pretty blonde who ought to know better."

"Now, now, *chiquita*, Jake, at the core, is nearly as jolly as you."

"Not tonight."

Gomez eased around her and walked through the nearly empty restaurant to the booth Jake was sharing with his son and Bev. "For lack of anything better to do," he explained as he slid onto the bench next to Jake, "I was monitoring the cop channels on my skycar dash and thus heard that some poor *hombre* was found dead on your doorstep. When I arrived on the scene, the amiable Drexler told me he'd shooed you elsewhere."

"Yeah, we were just starting to talk about what happened, Sid." He tapped his forefinger absently on the side of his plazmug of nearcaf. "You knew Pete Traynor, didn't you?"

"Much better than I wanted to. A *burrito*, stubborn and stupid—at least as far as Tek was concerned. You were wise, *amigo*, to cross that guy off your guest list." Gomez smiled across the table. "Evening, Bev. Daniel."

Dan nodded, smiling back. "I was filling them in on what I heard Traynor saying," he told Gomez. "I didn't share any of this with Lieutenant Drexler."

"He's not the sort of *pendejo* who invites sharing."

"I heard somebody shouting out there and I figured he was drunk or drugged on something," continued Dan, resting both elbows on the tabletop. "He—and I didn't catch everything—was talking to people, imaginary people. One name he yelled was Flanders. He said something about not having anything to do with what happened to this Flanders. And he called out to Amy. Oh, and somebody named Denton or Dennis."

Gomez asked, "Did you actually talk to him before he expired?"

"A little, yeah," answered Jake's son. "He'd been shouting Dad's name, too, which is why I went out to take a look. I recognized him and it was obvious something was wrong. He looked sick, disoriented. He knew who I was, too, and he told me it was important that he talk to you, Dad."

Jake asked, "He didn't say about what?"

Dan shook his head. "Well, he started to say something about some kind of hijacking. But he had that seizure—or whatever it was—and just died."

Bev put her arm around the young man's shoulders. "Rough thing for you to go through."

"Not that bad," said Dan. "It was all the cop activity afterwards that really got me upset, Bev."

Gomez waved away the copperplated waitress, who was heading for their booth with a drawn electronic orderpad. "Give me a few more minutes to gather my thoughts and order, dear lady."

"You got it, Sidney." She ground to a halt, tottered, and withdrew to the front of the cafe again.

"It sounds like they slipped this Tek addicted *hombre* a sizzler," observed Gomez.

Jake said, "That's what our chum Drexler thinks, too."

Gomez gave a shrug. "Even a nitwit can have a right notion occasionally," he said. "Traynor was apparently having hallucinations about things that were on his mind. I assume his nocturnal visit wasn't announced in advance."

"Nope, I had no idea he was coming by—and I don't know what he wanted to talk to me about." Jake leaned back, took a sip of his nearcaf. "In spite of his Tek habit, the guy was a pretty good weapons technician. Last I heard, he had a fairly responsible job with Gunsmiths, Ltd., out in the West Hills Sector."

"Those *cabróns* cook up a lot of the nastier weapons used by our esteemed nation—and for a whole stewpot of less esteemed countries around the globe—to extermi- nate their current shitlist entries," said Gomez, rubbing at his moustache. "Could it be that the late Pedro Traynor was agitated and het up about a hijacking of some of Gunsmith's engines of destruction?"

"Something stolen from an outfit like that," said Dan, "that could be dangerous all right."

"The thing is, Traynor's dead and gone," said Jake. "So we'll probably never find out."

Frowning thoughtfully, Bev said, "Flanders. We started working on a case a few weeks ago—my agency gets a case every so often, even though it's nowhere near as big as the Cosmos outfit you guys work for—a case in- volving a Wes Flanders, who was gunned down in the Casino Strip in the Hollywood Sector. He worked for the Banx Card central office. We haven't solved it yet and neither have the police. I'm wondering if he could be the Flanders your visitor was referring to."

"I didn't hear any first name," said Dan. "But this Flanders *was* killed recently and Traynor apparently thought somebody was trying to blame him."

"Is there a pattern here, folks?" inquired Gomez, making another shooing motion at the robot waitress, who seemed on the verge of rumbling toward their booth again. "A banker and a weapons technician—what's the link?"

"Probably isn't one," Jake said. "As for Amy—that has to be Amy St. Mars, Traynor's erstwhile missus."

"Of the St. Mars Ponics agriculture empire?" asked his partner, sitting up straighter. "There's a family with *dinero*."

"The same, yeah. They divorced about a year or more back. Traynor came to me to help him prove she wasn't treating their two kids right," said Jake, his fingers circling the mug. "He hoped to get custody from her—but I didn't want to get tangled up with anything like that. For one thing, it would've been impossible to prove he was any fitter a parent than Amy."

"Well, we've checked off most of the names you heard, Dan," commented Bev. "Except for Denton/Dennis. Anybody got a suggestion on him?"

Jake shook his head. "You know, why don't we simply forget all about this?" he suggested to them. "Traynor and I were a hell of a long way from being pals. Okay, he died—assassinated apparently—on my doorstep, but I sure don't feel any strong desire to avenge him. Unless it starts to look like Dan and I are in danger, I'd just as well back off completely from this mess."

Bev asked him, "Aren't you even curious, Jake?"

"Not especially, no. Tekheads are getting knocked off with considerable frequency in these parts."

Gomez said, "But usually not so close to your hearth and home, *amigo.*"

"Even so," said Jake. "I'd like to pass on this one. Especially since nobody is paying us to poke around and investigate."

After a few seconds, Gomez signaled to the robot waitress. "Long as we're here, I think I'll have a vegetarian fish sandwich," he decided.

4

The dark-haired young woman with the lazgun resting on her knee was thin, at least fifteen pounds underweight. She was sitting, slouched slightly, in a tin slingchair out on the shadowy deck in front of Jake's place when he got back from seeing Bev Kendricks home. It was nearly two AM; the law had long since departed and hauled away the body of Peter Traynor. The wind had died to a warm whisper.

"You're Jake Cardigan, aren't you?" she asked, not getting up.

He stepped onto the deck, eyes on the weapon she was holding. "Yeah, and you?"

She glanced down at the gun in her lap. "Oh, this is for my protection," she explained. "Not to use on you."

"Put it away anyhow." He moved closer to her.

Sliding the lazgun into a pocket of her black jacket, she said, "I'm Janine Traynor. Peter was my stepbrother." She brushed at her dark hair with a bony hand. "I want you to find out who killed him."

Light suddenly blossomed around the deck floor. Dan, a stungun in his right hand, stepped out into the night. "Everything all right, Dad?"

"Sure, just having a cordial chat with this young lady."

"Need me?"

"Not yet."

Nodding slowly, giving Janine a sideways look, Dan slipped back inside the apartment.

"I didn't know," mentioned Jake as he straddled a neowood chair, "that Pete had a sister."

"Stepsister."

"How old are you?"

"What the hell does that have to do with your finding out who murdered him?"

"Not a damn thing actually. Just curious."

She sighed, sniffling once. "I'm twenty one, okay," she said, touching at the pocket that held the gun. "I'm a vid actress—sometimes anyway, whenever my dimwitted agents can dig me up some work. That's part of what we have to talk over, Cardigan."

Jake said nothing, watching her.

"What I mean is," continued the dead man's sister, "I can't pay the kind of fee that Bascom and the Cosmos Detective Agency asks for."

"You know, huh, who I work for?"

"Obviously, for Christ's sake. I didn't come to you just because my brother happened to die in your vicinity," she told him. "Peter told me about you. That you were fairly honest and that he trusted you."

"You sound as though you, maybe, don't share in that appraisal of me."

She tilted her head to the left, studying him. Dan had left the floor lights on and the shadows beneath her eyes and cheekbones showed deep and sooty. "Not completely yet," she admitted finally. "You look trustworthy on the outside, but inside—who can tell?"

He grinned. "Gather yourself up and go home, then."

"No, I'll go on what my brother felt about you for now," Janine told him. "What I want you to do—Well, I'm pretty sure you can persuade that vindictive bitch who used to be his wife to finance an investigation into Peter's death."

"You didn't study diplomacy in school. Not a good idea to label people you're trying to get money out of as vindictive bitches."

"C'mon, Cardigan, you know damned well Amy St. Mars is a nasty shrew." She crossed her legs, uncrossed them, crossed them again. The knees were sharp, with too little flesh to them. "When you go to her, you obviously won't mention my true feelings or yours."

"You're suggesting that I lie and dissemble? That would tarnish my trustworthy image, wouldn't it?"

"Look, Cardigan, there's being twenty one and then there's being twenty one," she said slowly, angry. "The life I've led—Let's just say I'm not especially naive. I know you have to con people to get what you want. Now, please, let's get back to business."

"I don't think, Miss Traynor, we're going to be doing any business."

"Hey, I'm offering you a case. A goddamned job."

"Nope, you're telling me to go try and beg a fee off Pete's widow," he corrected. "Now, if you know as much about their relationship as you ought to, you know that Amy wouldn't pay ten bucks to keep wild dogs from pissing on his grave. She sure as hell isn't going to hire Cosmos and pay our kind of fees."

"She's got millions."

"People who have millions have millions, most of them, because they're extremely careful about how they spend any of those millions." He got up from his chair, wandered over to the deck rail to look out toward the dark ocean. "That's been my experience."

She left the slingchair and came to stand at his side. It was still warm, but she shuddered now and hugged herself. "I figured out where he died," she said, pointing. "Right about there."

"More or less."

"Aren't you at all interested in what happened to him?" she asked quietly. "He was your friend."

"He was somebody I knew a long time ago, that's all."

She reached over and touched his arm. "I know why he was coming to talk to you."

He turned to look at her. "Oh, so?"

"Peter and I haven't been especially close lately," Janine began. "I mean, he didn't think too much of some of the acting jobs I had to take—and he was annoyed because I kept after him to get himself, quick, into some kind of Tek rehab program." She lowered her head, sniffling again. "He was a bright man, a good person before he got all tangled up with that stuff."

"Get back to what Pete was so anxious to talk to me about."

"I'm coming to that," she said. "I want you to understand that I don't know as much as I should because we didn't see each other as often these past few weeks."

"Okay, go on."

"What I do know is that Peter was very upset about something that was going on at Gunsmiths, Ltd. He was working for them, you know."

"Yeah. Were weapons being stolen from there?"

"Did he tell you that tonight?"

"He didn't tell me a damn thing. He was dead and done for long before I got home."

"Maybe he told your son?"

"No, that was just a guess, Janine. Based on what you've been telling me."

"All right, I think he was worried about some sort of particularly dangerous weapon," she said, leaning an elbow on the rail and watching the surf glide in across the dark sand. "He hinted, without coming out directly, that a dangerous weapon was being smuggled out of Gunsmiths. Probably from their San Andreas Arsenal warehouse."

"What's kept there?"

"From what my brother told me, that's where they

stockpile stuff. And where they're supposed to mothball supplies of weapons that have been outlawed or put on hold because of UN rulings and such."

"He give you any specifics?" Jake took hold of her thin arm and guided her back toward the chair.

Shaking her head, she sat again. "All I know is that he was very scared," she said. "He suspected someone in the company—an important someone—was letting something important be taken out of the warehouse."

"You know anybody name Denton or Dennis?"

She patted the gun in her pocket again. "That might be Dennis Barragray," she answered. "He's one of the vice presidents at Gunsmiths, and a good friend of my brother's. Where'd you hear about him?"

Straddling the neowood chair, Jake asked her, "What about Wes Flanders?"

"I never heard of him. Is he somebody who worked at Gunsmiths, Ltd., with Peter?"

"Nope."

"Can we get back, then, to why I came to see you, Cardigan?" She folded her thin hands together. "Will you, please, take the case? It's important, not just to me, to find out who did this to my brother—and exactly why."

Jake said, "I work for the Cosmos agency, not myself, Janine. Walt Bascom isn't noted for sentimentality or generosity. If you want to hit Amy St. Mars on your own and persuade her to finance this—that's fine. Otherwise, this is all we have to talk about."

"That's a shitty attitude." Janine stood up, thrust her

hands deep into her jacket pockets. "Don't you give a damn what happened to him?"

"I'm sorry he's dead," he replied. "But I never do charity work. On top of which, it's one hell of a long time since I risked my ass for a cause."

"But I thought you believed in what you did."

"I'm a professional. I don't need faith." He nodded toward the night beach. "Where'd you park your skycar?"

"I took a skycab."

"I'll take you home."

"Don't strain your generosity."

"You want a lift or don't you?"

"Okay, all right. I'll accept the offer." She moved, slowly, across the deck. Turning, she looked, forlornly, back toward him. "I'm awfully disappointed."

"Happens a lot when you're young."

5

The morning was clear, pale blue and chilly. Jake was on the homeward lap of his daily run along the Malibu Sector beach. Out on the deck of an ivory white beach house two goldplated robots were setting out a large breakfast table and four chairs. One of the bots waved to Jake.

"Morning, Ralph," called Jake, returning the wave.

"Got time for a cup of nearcaf?" inquired the glittering mechanism.

"Not today."

Farther along Jake encountered a plump silver-haired young woman in a scarlet beach robe. She was squatting at the edge of the sea. "Darn, heck," she muttered as she poked a pudgy finger into the wet sand, probing for something.

"Problem, Jane?" Jake slowed and halted.

"Yeah, darn it," she answered, not looking up. "I lost my mood patch again."

"Shouldn't go swimming with that still on your arm." He crouched beside her.

"I wasn't swimming. Just doing my exercises." Jane kept on searching. "If I don't find the darn thing—it's my last one until I can get the prescription refilled—I'm going to swing from manic to depressed all day. I'll probably punch my halfwit boss at the Ponics Farmers' Market and then—"

"Here it is." Jake spotted the tiny silvery circle near his right foot. He picked it up carefully, blew off the sand and returned it to the anxious young woman.

"Great, thanks." Chuckling, she stood, rolled up her sleeve and slapped the mood-controlling disc in place on her upper arm. "By the way, who was that who got slaughtered in front of your digs last night, Jake?"

"Somebody I used to know."

"What in the devil killed the poor doof?"

Jake said, "Soon as the police tell me, I'll let you know." He resumed running.

Dan, dressed in his SoCal Police Academy uniform, was sitting out on the deck with a glass of citrisub in his hand. Molly Fine, also in uniform, was occupying the slingchair that the dead man's sister had used last night. Molly was slim and dark, a year older than Jake's son.

"Good morning, Jake. It's impressive how you can run

such a distance and not get all red in the face the way my Uncle Stan does after about fifty feet." She stood up, smiling at him. "I'm collecting your wayward son and giving him free transport to school this morning."

"I noticed your skycar parked there next to mine, Molly, and figured as much."

"See?" said Dan, setting his glass on the deck beside his chair. "I told you Dad was still an ace detective despite his advanced age. Give him just a little clue like a lemon yellow skycar and he—"

"Respect for your elders is something they ought to be teaching at the academy." Jake leaned an elbow on the rail.

Molly said, "Now—about the Gunsmiths outfit."

He glanced over at his son. "Been telling her all about—"

"I wheedled the information out of him," the young woman explained. "I'm pretty good at interrogation. I get better grades in that area than Dan, though maybe that isn't saying much."

"One of her uncles is—"

"Uncle Jerry," took up Molly. "He used to do legal work for Gunsmiths. Uncle Jerry's the one with the diminished capacity for integrity."

"Molly thinks she knows something about what's stored at the San Andreas Arsenal."

Nodding, she asked Jake, "Ever hear of Garret Devlin?"

"Technical whiz, no moral sense to speak of, killed in a skytram crash in New Phoenix three years ago."

"That's him, right. Devlin, according to what my disreputable attorney uncle once told me, was a specialist in creating all sorts of nasty weapons," she said. "Weapons that were so nasty, in fact, most of them were outlawed before ever getting used in combat."

"And that's part of what's being stored in the warehouse?"

"Yeah, along with a lot of other deadly stuff," said Molly. "If some of Devlin's gadgets have been hijacked or smuggled out of there—well, havoc, destruction and worse may be in the offing, Jake."

He said, "Dan probably didn't mention that I have no connection, official or otherwise, with this whole business. I'm making a serious effort to forget all about Peter Traynor, his employers and his stepsister."

"Gomez," observed Dan, nodding skyward.

The detective's skycar was drifting down through the brightening morning. It settled smoothly to a landing next to Molly's vehicle. Gomez, wearing a jacket the color of a tropical sunrise, emerged. "Get out of your sports togs and into your work duds," he advised. "*Buenas dias*, Molly. You're looking even lovelier than when we last met."

"That was only four nights ago, Gomez," she said as he came bounding onto the deck. "At the Twentieth Century Jazz Android Orchestra concert over in the Hollywood Sector."

The curlyhaired detective took her hand, bent and kissed it. "It must be that your charm is increasing at an alarming rate, *chiquita*."

"Trust him," said Dan. "He's an expert on female charm."

"I know, I've read his dossier." She retrieved her hand. "Five wives."

Gomez frowned at his partner. "Have I, truly, been married five times?"

"I quit counting after three. Why am I supposed to change clothes?"

"Bascom, our beloved *jefe*, wants to see us both *muy pronto*," he explained. "He vidphoned me to swing by and gather you up. We have a meeting with an important client in about thirty minutes or so."

"What sort of a case?"

"You'll be pleased to hear," answered his partner with a smile, "that we're being hired to investigate the murder of the late Peter Traynor."

"A SISTER, EH?" Gomez was hunched slightly in the drive seat of his skycar.

"A very intense and sincere sister, yeah," answered Jake as they flew toward the Cosmos Detective Agency building in the Laguna Sector of Greater LA. "Or so she tried to seem."

"*Ai*, you're becoming ever more cynical with each passing day, *amigo*."

"Janine Traynor is an actor," said Jake. "Sometimes actors tend to act even off stage."

"She was very convincing, though?"

"Yeah, and the tears were real." Jake then filled him in

on what the young woman had told him last night and also on the footnote on Gunsmiths, Ltd., that Molly had added this morning.

"So just about all the names Pedro was yelling during his last go-round with Tek are tied in with that weapons factory."

"Except for Amy and Wes Flanders."

"Wouldn't have been too tough for you to have found out how Flanders connects." Gomez punched out a landing pattern on the dash controls. "Since Bev is working on that case involving him, she would've shared enough information for you to track—"

"Last night, remember, I'd resolved not to poke around in this business."

"You can't fight fate. We're apparently destined to investigate this one," observed the detective. "Bev—have I mentioned this?—is an impressive lady. You ought to see more of her—maybe even ask her to go steady."

The skycar settled down on the roof landing area of one of the Cosmos towers.

"What you haven't mentioned is who our client is." Jake stepped free of the car.

"I was saving the news," said Gomez. "It is none other than the onetime spouse, Amy St. Mars."

Jake frowned, shaking his head. "Looks like Janine is a lot more persuasive than I figured."

6

Bascom's suit was almost presentable, his vast desk was only moderately disordered, and he even seemed to have fewer wrinkles on his weathered, tanned face. "Gents, I trust all is well with you?" he inquired as the partners entered his tower office. All the windows were unblanked this morning and the big circular room was full of sunshine.

Gomez slacked his pace, taking hold of Jake's arm. "*Amigo*, I think this must be a cleverly constructed android sim of our respected *padrone*," he announced. "The Walt Bascom I serve so devotedly ain't anywhere near this cheerful of a morning."

"Yeah, and this impostor isn't rumpled and wrinkled enough to be our esteemed boss."

"Sit down and spare me any further schoolboy wit." Bascom nodded at a couple of chairs near his desk. "I don't see why you yahoos can't accept the fact that I've changed for the better."

As Gomez sank into his plazchair, he said, "You see what the love of a good woman can do, Jake?"

Jake straddled his chair, watching the chief. "You still courting Kay Norwood?"

"The attorney and I are good friends, lads," he conceded. "We'll be visited by our client, by way of holographic projection, in a little less than eight minutes. Suppose, Jake, you tell me about that fracas at your place last evening. I've already scanned the police reports."

Jake obliged, concluding with, "What's Amy told you?"

"Not a damn thing beyond the size of the fee she's willing to fork over." Bascom walked over to sit on the edge of the hologram projection stage. "I had to cajole her into offering us anywhere near what we're worth. She's one of the richest ladies in SoCal, yet a shade on the parsimonious side."

"Somebody," said Jake, "was mentioning to me recently that detectives should work simply for the love of seeing justice done."

"Sure, yep, justice is nice," admitted the head of the detective agency. "A fat fee is better."

Gomez smiled. "We can have that inscribed on your tombstone, *jefe*."

"I'm going to be cremated and leave instructions to blow my ashes in the eyes of several assholes who've been less than sweet to me during my stay on earth." A faint buzzing hum started under his backside. Bascom jumped up and patted a keypad on the stage. "This will be the grieving widow."

A very believable image of a pretty, slender woman of thirty five appeared on the stage. She was sitting in a silvery metal chair and her long red hair was tied back with a single strand of black ribbon. "Good morning, Jake," Amy St. Mars said in her husky voice. "You look much the worse for wear. Apparently being on ice up in the Freezer didn't do you any good."

"You're as lovable as ever, Amy." He moved his chair so he faced her projected image.

"No wiseassing with the clients," advised Bascom in a whisper.

"That's perfectly all right, Bascom." She leaned forward and rested the palm of her right hand on her right knee. She was wearing a simple white frock, slit to the thigh. "Jake and I, as I'm sure he's told you by now, are old friends. I used to run into him on the many occasions when I was dragging my former husband out of various Tek joints."

"Jake has reformed long since," Bascom assured her.

"Oh, I'm well aware of that or I wouldn't be hiring you people at all. I won't have a damn thing to do with Tekheads." She rubbed at her knee. "Can we get down to business now? I have to be in Frisco in two hours. Let me commence by explaining that I have absolutely no feelings for Peter. He was a hopeless Tekkie, a pain in the ass, and he's better off dead." She straightened up, moved her hand to her left knee. "He was, long ago, fairly attractive and charming, and before he cooked his brains with Tek, he had a relatively good mind. Yet one of the happiest days in my young life was the one on which our dreadful marriage was over for good."

Jake moved his chair about two feet forward. "So you're not exactly hiring Cosmos to avenge Pete's death?"

She gave a slow shake of her head. "No, Jake," she answered. "If he'd died of natural causes or been killed in some sort of accident, well, hell, I wouldn't even send flowers to the bastard. What concerns and upsets me is that someone hastened his end. He *was* murdered, wasn't he?"

"That he was," confirmed Bascom. "I got hold of the initial coroner's report—the one done up by the prelim robots—right after you called to set up this appointment, Miss St. Mars. It was a sizzler that killed him. A sizzler is a Tek chip that—"

"I know what it is, Bascom," she cut in disdainfully. "I was, remember, married to a Tekkie." She rubbed at her left knee. "About the only admirable thing Peter ever did was father our two children. Alex is just ten and Marisa will be seven and, praise the lord, neither one of them is a bit like him. I'm extremely fond of both of them and I make sure I spend at least a full half hour with them every day."

"Mother love," muttered Gomez, "you can't beat it."

"I was wondering how long it'd be before you popped off, Gomez," said Amy. "You were a wiseass when you were with the SoCal cops, too. But be quiet for a while and let me get on with this."

"Hush," mentioned Bascom, giving the curlyhaired detective a sour look.

"I've upped the security on all three of our homes," continued Amy. "I'm confident that we're all safe when we're at home, but the kids have to go out to school every day and I travel a great deal for St. Mars Ponics. I've added bodyguards, too, but I feel we're still vulnerable. I have very little confidence in the police and I'll feel a lot better once the killers are caught."

"Killers?" asked Bascom. "Plural?"

"I assume this is some kind of conspiracy thing," Amy told them. "And I'm very concerned that they may suspect I know more than I do. Peter paid the children a monthly visit—I had to concede that when I got rid of him." She sighed out a slow breath, inhaled slowly. "The last time I saw him—which was at our Studio City Sector home three weeks ago—he told me he was afraid he was in serious trouble because of some knowledge he'd stumbled across. If these people who killed him think that I know what he knew—or that he might even have told the children something—they'll try to harm us, too."

"What sort of trouble was he in, *señorita?*"

"Why are we speaking Spanish, for God's sake?" She gave Gomez an annoyed frown before going on. "Peter, as you know, was employed by Gunsmiths, Ltd. As a matter of fact, I helped him get the job a few years back by putting in a word with a close, dear friend of mine, Dennis Barragray." She paused, shaking her head. Part of the black hair ribbon came loose. "Peter didn't provide me a great many details and, I have to admit, I wasn't paying close attention to what he was nattering about. But it had something to do with a shipment of weapons that he suspected was taken, on the sly, from the San Andreas Arsenal warehouse facilities. Peter, fool that he was, was also digging into how this supposed smuggling operation was financed."

"Wes Flanders." Jake snapped his fingers. "Did your husband know him?"

"*Former* husband," she quickly corrected. "Yes, Wes Flanders—another Tekhead, by the way—was a good friend of Peter's. In fact, Flanders was killed recently, too. That unsettled Peter a great deal."

Bascom was standing over by his big desk now. He absently tapped on the bell of his saxophone, which was sprawled atop several neat stacks of faxmemos. "Who'd Traynor suspect was involved with whatever the hell was going on at Gunsmiths, Ltd.?"

"I don't know that," she replied. "I do know he mentioned some of these suspicions of his to Dennis. Dennis thought Peter was simply suffering from a Tek hangover—but, obviously, he was onto something."

Jake asked, "Did Pete have any idea where these highjacked weapons were ending up?"

"If he did, he didn't mention it to me."

"Anything about what kind of weapons specifically?"

"Pete said, as best I can recall, something about the Devlin Gun. Does that mean anything?"

"Bingo," said Gomez.

"It does, yeah," Jake told her. "At least, it might. Garret Devlin was in charge of Research & Development at Gunsmiths until his death three years back. He came up with some pretty deadly—and often illicit—weapons in his time."

"Peter knew too much about that and they killed him," Amy said, putting both hands together and entangling her slender fingers. "If they think I know something, too . . ." She stiffened in her silver chair. "I expect rapid and positive results from Cosmos, Bascom."

"You'll get 'em." Bascom was standing straight, smiling stiffly at the holographic image. "And more, to boot."

"You haven't talked at all about Traynor's stepsister," put in Jake. "But I guess she was able to enlist your help."

"Beg pardon?"

"I'm referring to Janine Traynor."

Impatience sounded in Amy St. Mars's voice as she said, "Peter never had a sister, step or otherwise." She stood up. "He was, Jake, an only child." Her image vanished from the room.

7

Bascom turned away from the vidphone on his desk as the screen went black. "Well, lads," he said, "the minions of the law haven't made much further progress."

Gomez was sunk in a bubblechair. "The final autopsy confirms that Pedro was bumped off with a sizzler Tek chip," he remarked. "So there's one item for our travel itinerary. We have to find out where he was slipped that fatal Tek *and* on whose orders."

"Cops haven't been able to determine yet what joint he visited before dropping in at Jake's last night," said the agency head. "I want us to solve this ahead of them. If Traynor really did know something about an international gunrunning plot—I can finagle a nice bonus from one of the relatively honest US government agencies I am cozy with."

"Crass. Everybody in Greater LA is so crass," sighed Gomez. "It really pains a sensitive youth such as myself."

Jake was at one of the high, wide windows, watching the midmorning outside. Absently, he followed the upward progress of a scarlet skybus that was rising up from its stop platform. "Who the hell was posing as his sister?" he said.

Bascom picked up his saxophone. "That," he said, "is certainly something you have to find out, my boy."

"Now, if she had visited me," offered Gomez, "we could figure that her yarn about being kin of the deceased was merely a flimsy excuse to get close to one of the most charming *hombres* in all of Greater Los Angeles." He shrugged one shoulder. "But love struck maidens aren't in the habit of throwing themselves at Jake."

"The few that do don't need excuses." Jake went over and sat on the edge of the holo platform. "Janine Traynor, whoever she really may be, wanted to find out how much I knew—how much Pete told me before he died. That has to be what she was up to."

"Or maybe," put in Gomez, "she really and truly does want to find out who knocked off the poor guy."

"Meaning what—that she's actually a ladyfriend of his?"

"It's possible, *amigo*."

"I'll find out."

Bascom rested the sax across his knees. "It would also be nice to know what the late Wes Flanders was nosing around in," he suggested. "And whether he and Traynor were collaborating on some kind of halfass investigation."

Gomez unslouched slightly. "Dillinger," he said toward Jake.

"I'll talk to him, yeah," he said. "First, though, I want to see what Bev has on Flanders."

"Who might Dillinger be?" inquired the agency head.

"*Jefe*, you don't keep up with who's who in informers, stool pigeons, snitches and blabbermouths." Gomez sunk farther down into the fat yellow chair. "Dillinger is a young chap who specializes in accessing privileged banking information."

Nodding, Bascom frowned in Jake's direction. "I don't, you know, want folks getting the impression we have to go running to some little pipsqueak detective outfit for help."

"*Cuidado*," cautioned Gomez with a smile, "careful. You're speaking of the pipsqueak he loves."

The chief put the saxophone back on his desk. "You and Bev Kendricks are an item?"

"We're friends," said Jake evenly. "And if you don't approve of how I handle my work, Walt, maybe it's time for me to quit this damn outfit and—"

"Whoa, hey, easy," said Bascom, holding up his right hand in a stop-right-there motion. "I retract anything I said that's annoyed you."

Jake was on his feet now. "I have to be able to work in any way I think is —"

"Let's make a list of chores for today, gang." Gomez stood up. "Me, I'll find out which Tek parlor Traynor visited and, hopefully, who slipped him the sizzler and why. You want to follow up on the Flanders business first, Jake?"

After a few seconds his partner replied, "I'll start with that, yeah."

"*Bueno*. Later in the day I'll check with you and we'll compare notes on what fun we've had thus far," said Gomez. "What about the folks at Gunsmiths, Ltd.? Do we waltz right in or do we use an oblique approach?"

Bascom answered, "By now, they probably know we're on the case. So, initially anyway, walk right in on the bastards and start asking questions."

"Dennis Barragray is the first one to talk to," said Jake. "He was Traynor's boss and a friend of his. He's also a friend of our client, so you ought to be able to see him without too much trouble."

"I'll grill him, " offered Gomez. "My first inquiry will be—'Did you slip Pedro a sizzler because he had the goods on you?' That ought to start the ball rolling, don't you think?"

"Be just a wee bit subtler," advised his chief.

Jake moved to the door. "I'll be in touch, Sid." He left the big office.

Bascom frowned as the door hissed shut. "Jake seems to be pissed off at me," he observed.

"Terrific deduction, *jefe*." Gomez headed for the way out. "We'll be able to make a detective of you yet."

8

The simulated canals down at this end of the Venice Sector of Greater LA were not, as usual, in especially good shape. The water was a cloudy yellow and reeked of decay and worse. As Gomez walked along the ground-level pedramp, he noted a dead calico cat and a partly burned toyboat go floating, sluggishly, by. "Scenic wonders abound," he murmured, increasing his pace.

Farther up the bedraggled block a rusty, dented robot was sitting crouched in the doorway of a shut-down wineshop. Taped to the rattletrap mechanical man's pocked copper chest was a hand-lettered sign—*My friends, I was once the valet of a prominent vid superstar. Ill fortune and failing ratings ruined his career and, thus, mine. I*

*lost my position and, after a pathetic series of humiliating fail-
ures, ended up in this slew of despond that you find me in at
present. However, an expensive tune-up will put me on my feet
again. God bless you for whatever you see your way clear to
contributing.*

"You misspelled slough," mentioned Gomez in passing.

The seated bot eyed him with dingy plazeyes. "You
making a contribution, sir?"

"No, merely a correction in your pitch."

"Then go blurp yourself."

"Blurp?"

"I was a very proper gentleman's gentleman, programmed to use no seriously vulgar language, sir. You
walleyed poop."

Smiling, the detective moved onward.

At the corner he found the establishment he was seek-
ing. Lettered in gloletters across the dusty, narrow shop
window was *Fragrant Illusions* and below that *The BEST
in Holographic Flowers.* Gomez, frowning, noticed that all
the dozen or so brick-red flowerpots on display in the
window were devoid of flowers, holographic or otherwise.

Cautiously, he entered the shop. "What happened to
your blooms?" he asked the handsome blond android
clerk who stood behind the narrow counter.

The andy made no reply. He remained standing stiffly,
arms at his sides, eyes staring.

"*Cuidado,*" Gomez warned himself as he drew out his
stungun from its shoulder holster beneath his jacket.

After a moment, he moved across the room and stopped in front of the rear door. The door was a few inches open.

He listened for several seconds, then booted the door all the way open and hopped to one side.

"Come on in, Gomez," invited a voice from the next room.

THE FIGHT DIDN'T start until Jake had been there for nearly ten minutes. Bev's offices were in the Santa Monica Sector, in a tall, mostly plastiglass building that was built out over the Pacific. At midmorning there was still a thin white mist hanging over the quiet blue water. Gulls were diving into the white blur, disappearing and reappearing.

"There's nobody we've turned up in the Flanders case who fits the description of this Janine Traynor," Bev was saying from behind her desk.

Jake turned his back to the window. "Then she was connected in some other way," he said. "Have you connected Flanders with Traynor yet?"

"I'm following up on that," the blonde detective said. "So far this killing looked to me like a typical Tek assassination. But we can't come up with any reason for the Teklords to want to eliminate Flanders. He didn't seem that important till now."

"I'd like to go over your files on Flanders," he said. "Unless that violates agency policy."

"It's my agency, Jake," she reminded him.

"To my way of thinking, both killings must have some-

thing to do with what's going on wrong out at Gunsmiths." Jake sat in a metallic chair that faced her desk.
"But some of the Tek cartels have to be tied in, too. Both
of them were killed with traditional Tek methods."

"Could also be a copycat."

He shook his head negatively. "Nope, feels to me like
there has to be a Tek angle someplace."

Bev smiled. "Hunches don't always stand up."

"Even so." He leaned forward in his chair. "If you're
going to dig into the links between Flanders and Traynor, I'll concentrate on some of the other aspects of this
mess. Then later we can compare—"

The door to Beth's private office came hissing open
and a large, wide man of thirty five or so came barging
in. His face was flushed with anger, both big fists were
clutched. "What the hell is this bastard doing here?
Damn it now, Bev, you can't—"

"What I can or can't do is no business of yours, Jabb,"
she said evenly. "If you want to see me, wait until—"

"What I have to talk about," said Jabb Marx, pointing
angrily at Jake, "is this asshole here. It's bad enough you
see him socially, for Christ sake, but now you're sharing
confidential agency files with him."

"How do you know I'm sharing anything with him?"

"It's obvious that's why he's here—to pump you about
the Wes Flanders case."

Jake had risen to his feet. "Marx," he said quietly, "get
out of here now."

"You just keep the hell quiet, Cardigan," the detective
shouted at him. "I tell you something, asshole—you got

one good woman killed so far in your career, but I'm damned if I'm going to let the same thing happen to Bev."

Jake didn't say anything. He was just all at once next to Marx. He hit him, hard, in the midsection.

Marx gasped, doubled, tried to swing at Jake.

Jake kicked him, his booted foot connected with his ribs.

Marx jerked back, clutching at his side, groaning.

Jake moved in, hitting him again and again in the face with each fist in turn.

His face bloody, his jacket and shirt splotched with red, Marx dropped to his knees.

Jake kicked him again, in the chest this time.

"Jake!" cried Bev.

The woman may have cried out before, but Jake hadn't been hearing anything for a while there.

"Jake." She ran over to him, caught him by an arm and pulled him back. "That's enough—more than enough."

Jake shook himself, as though he'd just stepped out of the chill ocean. "Sorry," he managed to croak. His voice was raw, raspy.

Pushing him aside, she knelt next to the unconscious operative. "His nose is broken, lord knows what else is wrong." She reached up and flipped a switch on the voxbox on her desk. "Emmy Lou, get the medibots up here—quick!"

"He was right," Jake said, his voice still not his own. "It's my fault that Beth died."

She stood up, spun and glared at him. "I don't give a

good goddamn who's right and who's wrong," she said, angry. "You don't have the right to do things like this."

"Maybe not." He shook his head once, left to right, before walking out of there.

DETECTIVE LIEUTENANT DREXLER said, "Too, late, Gomez."

"So I notice." He walked over to where the large, fat corpse was sprawled in front of the entrance to one of the Tek parlor cribs. "*Sí*, this is the proprietor, Lorenzo Printz, sure enough."

"The boss himself."

"I note they used a lazgun on the *cabrón*." There was a large sooty hole in the back of the sinsilk floral robe that was twisted around the huge puffy dead man. "Rather than a sizzler."

"Lorenzo, like most Tek joint operators, never touched the stuff." The black cop was sitting on the edge of a wooden chair. "How'd you find your way here, by the way?"

"Came in to buy a bunch of holo roses for my sweet old grandmother on her graduation from robotics night school," Gomez told him. "Much to my surprise, I found that somebody had used a stunner on the handsome clerk. Curious, I—"

"C'mon, don't make me treat you the way I treat that partner of yours. Tell me the truth—or at least part of it."

"Okay, we're working on the Traynor case." Gomez left the vicinity of the body.

"That I heard earlier in the day. How'd you end up at Lorenzo's Tek parlor here?"

"It's the one Traynor visited on his last night out. I was planning to persuade Lorenzo to confide in me."

"Who tipped you that this was the place Traynor'd been coming lately?"

Gomez smiled, settling into a chair near the policeman's. "I hope this won't change the warm feelings you have for me, Drexler, but I don't ever give out the names of my sources of information."

Drexler watched him for a moment. "And I suppose you don't know anything about who ordered Lorenzo to slip Traynor a sizzler?"

"Would I be here if I did? This was my first stop on the road to enlightenment," he said. "Any notions of your own?"

Drexler laughed. "I'll write up everything I know and send it to you."

"Everything okay back there?" called a female voice from out front.

"The forensic bots here, Cathleen?"

"They came with me, yes." A plump blonde young woman, uniformed, stepped into the Tek parlor. She wrinkled her nose upon sighting Gomez. "You going to haul Gomez off to the pokey, lieutenant?"

"*Chiquita*, after all we've meant to each other—how can you think I'd commit any sort of illegal act?" He left the chair.

"I'd toss him in a cell," she advised Drexler.

"No, no," he said. "Gomez has promised to cooperate

with us. Every single clue he unearths, he's going to turn over to the SoCal police."

"Oh, *sí*." He crossed to the doorway. "I'll even have them giftwrapped." He stepped across the threshold. "*Adiós*, colleagues."

Outside, he went striding toward the lot where he'd left the agency skycar.

9

When the vidphone on the dash of his skycar buzzed, Jake hit the auto/answer key.

A mechanical version of his voice said, "Please leave your message now."

Bev appeared on the small rectangular screen. She was seated at her desk, face pale, hands folded. "Jake, Jabb Marx will be spending the day at the Santa Monica Emergency Center," she said. "I'm pretty sure I've persuaded him not to take any legal action against you for assault. For now—well, I think you ought to stay away from me and the office. We'll be better off working separately on this Flanders-Traynor business for a while. I'll . . . I'll probably get in touch with you again in a couple of days." Then her image was gone from the screen.

After a moment Jake said aloud, "I'm not getting off to a very impressive start on this case."

"Beg pardon, sir?" inquired the voice of the car computer.

"Nothing. Talking to myself."

"Would you care to have me patch you through to one of the agency therapists?"

"Not just yet."

The computer said, "You have been, if I may mention it, unusually tense of late, sir. Is there anything I can do?"

"I appreciate your interest," said Jake. "But I don't think I'm far enough around the bend to need advice from my car. But thanks."

"As you wish, sir." The computer fell silent.

Jake punched out a flight pattern that would take him to the Palm Springs Sector.

GOMEZ TOOK A careful step backward, made a go-away motion with both hands. "I don't want to take a card."

The magician doll was nearly three feet high, dressed in a glittery tuxsuit and top hat. He had a perpetual grin under his slick, dark moustache. "Don't be a schmuck," he urged, fanning out six bright playing cards. "Take one, for Pete's sake."

"Hey, simp," said a fuzzy teddybear, jumping off his low perch, "ignore that four-flusher. Buy me. I'm the cutest darn toy in this whole darn Wondersmith's toyshop."

"You do have an awfully cute lisp," the detective admitted. "But I came to consult with your boss."

The bear, who was slightly shorter than the magician, came up closer to Gomez. "I remember you now, palsy walsy," he said accusingly. "Sure, you've been here before and you didn't buy a single toy then either."

"That's enough, guys. Get back on your pedestals." A large, fat woman with bright silvery hair came lumbering in from the office of the toyshop. "Hiya, Gomez, honey. Excuse these lovable little darlings."

"Lovable ain't one of the words, I'd apply, Corky."

"Up your nose," muttered the bear while climbing back onto his perch.

Corky Keepnews said, "Language, language. C'mon in, honey." She was clad in a sinsilk slaxsuit of a floral pattern similar to the one he'd recently seen on the dead man's robe.

Her toyshop office was in the Westwood Sector, up on the seventeenth level. From her one narrow viewindow you could see part of University of SoCal Campus #26, where either a riot or a rally was in progress in the glade.

"Found out anything yet?" he asked, watching Corky sink down into an immense armchair.

"Honey, am I not one of the best sources of information in the entire state?"

"I'll award you the title *after* you tell me something." He gingerly lifted a goldenhaired babydoll off a chair and sat.

"Watch who you're grabbing, kiddo," warned the doll in a small, piping voice.

He dropped her on the floor. "Well, Corky?"

"This, it turns out, is a seven-hundred-and-fifty-dollar job, hon."

"What's the extra two-fifty for?"

She turned away from him, watching the sunbright campus far below. "What the hell are you messed up with this time, sweetie?"

"You tell me. That's what this outrageous fee is for."

"After you phoned me to tell me that poor Lorenzo had shuffled off," began the silverhaired informant, "I commenced making some discreet inquiries for you. And it's a damn good thing I am so discreet. Otherwise, I'd be on somebody's shitlist myself."

"This buildup is very exciting, *bonita*, yet singularly uninformative."

"Putz," muttered the sprawled babydoll.

Gomez rested the sole of his boot on the back of the doll. "Continue, Corky."

"Okay, I wasn't able to find out who hired Lorenzo— rest his soul—to slip your boy Traynor that sizzler," the fat woman told him. "However, I did find out more than enough to scare the puckey out of me."

Gomez made an impatient noise.

Corky went on. "I do have a pretty good notion who hired the heavies to get rid of Lorenzo. The guys who did the job are local, honey, but the fee, a hefty one, came from Europe."

"*Caramba*." Gomez nodded. "That's an unexpected angle. Can you pin it down any, Cork? Europe, last time I dropped in, was a *big* place."

She looked away from him. "Spain," she said quietly.

"Ah, I see why you're uneasy." He narrowed his left eye, watching her. "We're talking about the Zabicas Cartel, aren't we, Corky?"

"You said it, I didn't."

"All right, so what's Carlos Zabicas interest, way over there in Madrid, in a local like Peter Traynor?"

"Nobody's saying a damn thing about your pal Traynor," said Corky, shifting uneasily in her big chair. "All I know is, the Spanish were the ones who hired Lorenzo done in. Could be, Gomez honey, it doesn't have anything to do with this Traynor."

"You rarely encounter coincidences in this dodge, Cork," he pointed out. "Lorenzo apparently slips Traynor a lethal dose of Tek. The very next day he's dispatched to glory, too. Naw, whoever had him bumped off, also is behind the Traynor knock off. And that person is, for reasons yet to be determined, none other than Carlos Zabicas."

"I'm thinking of taking a little vacation jaunt up to NorCal, honey," she informed him. "Can I have my seven-fifty right now on the spot?"

"There'll be an equal amount if you get me more on what Zabicas is up to."

She shook her head. "Nope, no," she said, continuing to shake her head. "There are some mean and nasty Teklords in these parts, Gomez, but compared to Zabicas they're as sweet as that goldenhaired babydoll under your foot. No, I am not going to risk having him hear about me."

Gomez said, "One thousand dollars."

"I can't, hon, just can't. I'll be vacationing for at least the next two weeks."

Gomez accidentally stepped down on the doll when he got up. "*Bueno*, Corky," he said. "For now—"

"Watch where you park the gunboats," complained the doll.

"Sorry, *chiquita*." He fished $750 in Banx chits out of an inside jacket pocket. "Contact me if you have a change of mind."

She grabbed the money. "That won't happen," she assured him.

10

From out of the voxbox on the skycar dash came Gomez's voice. "Hey, *amigo*," he said, "I know that vehicle of your isn't flying around up there all by itself. Answer me, *por favor.*"

Jake tapped the *talk* key. "Okay, invade my privacy."

On the phonescreen Gomez raised an eyebrow. "Why are you sulking?"

"I'll explain later, Sid. Found out anything?"

Nodding, Gomez answered, "The order to wipe out Peter Traynor originated over in sunny Spain."

"From somewhere in Madrid or environs?"

"Exactly. Oh, and they knocked off Lorenzo Printz early this morning over in the sunny Venice Sector," added his partner. "He was the *hombre* who provided the rigged Tek chip."

Jake's skycar began to drop down for a landing at the parking area on the outskirts of the Palm Springs Sector. It was midday now, hot and bright.

Jake asked, "Why would the Zabicas Cartel care about Pete?"

"When I put that very question to my source of information, she started packing her bags and implied she didn't want to pursue that particular line of inquiry any further."

"Can this be as simple as illicit weapons being smuggled from Gunsmiths to Zabicas?"

"My feeling, *amigo*, is that it's a lot more complicated than that," said Gomez. "But Carlos Zabicas and his henchmen are tangled up in something nasty that probably has to do with an engine of destruction like this fabled Devlin Gun."

"We'll have to find out a hell of a lot more about that gun, too."

"I intend to inquire about it when I call on Señor Barragray out at the Gunsmiths offices this afternoon."

The skycar glided groundward, settled to a landing in an empty slot in the parking area, rocking very slightly. "Looks like I'm in the Palm Springs Sector, Sid," said Jake. "I've got an appointment with Dillinger. You have anything else to pass along?"

"*Nada* right now," said Sid. "You don't want to share the cause of your gloom with me?"

"Later maybe."

"Okay, keep in touch," said Gomez. "Oh, and Lieutenant Drexler sends his warmest personal regards. *Adiós*."

DILLINGER LIVED IN an old orange trailer on the edge of town. The patch of sandy, weedy ground immediately in front of his place was cluttered with ugly, prickly cactus stuck in squat, gaudy ceramic pots and stunted little elves and gnomes made of earth-colored clay. Dillinger himself, an android, was sitting out in a faded canvas chair just to the left of the doorway. He was thin, looked like a thirty five year old. He had a thin, snide smile, a seedy old-fashioned straw hat tilted at a cocky angle on his head and yellow hightop shoes. His suit was a dusty white and it glowed in the hot desert sunlight. He was drinking beer out of a chilled old-fashioned brown glass bottle.

"Hi, chump," he greeted Jake as he approached the run-down trailer.

"You can actually guzzle that stuff, huh?"

"You bet, pal. I'm an electronics marvel. I can even piss." He smiled thinly. "So what can I do you for?"

"Someone who can build an andy as good as you, ought to be building something better than—"

"No preaching on the premises, jocko. Besides, hey, it ain't none of your beeswax." He took another swig of cold beer, smiled his smug smile up at his visitor. "What's your pleasure, chum?"

"Unfortunately, Dillinger, you're the best man in this particular trade or otherwise I'd—"

"Not *man*, jerk. Don't go anthropomorphizing me, pliz."

"Okay, I want to trace some transactions."

"That'll be five hundred smackers in front, sheik." He held out his dirty left hand, palm up.

"Afterwards."

"Nuts to you."

Jake dug out $250 in Banx chits. "Half now."

"Three hundred dollars."

"Two-fifty tops or I go to your nearest rival."

"Geeze, what a tightwad you are." Dillinger sighed out a beery breath. "And, hey, I know the size of the fees those lamebrain clients fork over to your detective agency."

Jake dropped the money on the android's hand. "There's a guy named Wes Flanders who—"

"*Was* a guy, past tense. Flanders, so I hear, has been pushing up daisies for some weeks now, pal."

"You knew him?"

Dillinger smiled. "I have an interest in the financial world, chum. I keep up with the vital statistics."

"You have any idea what he was up to?"

"He was up to no good." Dillinger laughed, winking up at Jake. "Wait out here while I pop into the villa and grab a lapper."

Jake watched a grey lizard, who was perched atop an elf, bask in the hot sun.

Dillinger returned swinging a greasy old-fashioned laptop computer. "This is an authentic antique—except for the snazzy modifications I built into her."

"You didn't do the work."

"Well, my creator, then," admitted the android. He settled into the faded canvas chair and spread the computer across his knees. "We have what the doubledomes refer to as a symbiotic relationship, however. So it's okay, get me, for me to take credit."

"I'd be interested in meeting the other half of your team."

Dillinger laughed a dry, nasty laugh. "Sure, next time it snows down in Hell, I'll give you a jingle, pal."

"Let's get back to Flanders." Jake dragged an old tin oil drum away from the side of the trailer and sat on it, watching the android.

"I got to nosing around in his affairs a few weeks back, when I heard he'd been bumped off," explained Dillinger, running his fingers over the keypad. "Let's return to him once again. Okay, are you paying attention? Flanders, who was a minor league player when it came to tracking financial data, was trying to trace some kale that came from Spain to Portugal to the Barbados to Manhattan and ended up here in good old SoCal."

"How much money are we talking about?"

"Twenty-five million dollars."

"An impressive sum."

"Drop in the bucket to most of the ginks involved, but interesting nevertheless."

"Where'd it start—in Madrid?"

"That's what Flanders thought—but that's because he didn't get a chance to trace it any further back before they gunned him down in the street," said the android, chuckling. "Plus which, he was sort of a dope and maybe he never would've tumbled onto the truth. But they didn't take any chances."

"Okay, so where did the money originate?"

"We'll get to that in a minute, pal. First, though, let me explain where it ended up."

"Somewhere in the vicinity of a Gunsmiths exec."

"Not exactly," said Dillinger with a thin smile. "I traced the sly investigations that Wes Flanders thought he was making—and, believe you me, the guy left a trail a mile wide—and he had the same hunch as you about this dough. Actually, though, pal, the whole wad ended up in the Gunsmiths, Ltd., Employees Scholarship Fund."

"Twenty five million is a big sum to hide in a scholarship fund. You sure, Dillinger?"

Reaching up with his dingy left hand, the android tilted his old straw hat to an even jauntier angle. "You know, don't you, how come I can ferret out the sort of financial dope that I do, Cardigan? It's because I got access to a lot of good cheat codes. The little formulas that the smart boys who design these so-called foolproof systems build in so they can sneak a gander whenever they feel like it. Don't ask me how I come by this stuff, because that's, like the feller says, a trade secret." He rested his fingers on the keypad. "I can get anything that Banx knows and I can sneak into about eighty percent of all the other financial facilities in the entire—"

"Impressive, but I'm already a loyal customer, Dillinger," Jake reminded him. "No need to sell me."

"I enjoy bragging, though, it's part of my nature," said

the android. "The point of the narrative is, pal, that when I tell you the kale was dumped in that scholarship fund account, you can take it as gospel."

"And who can draw on that particular account?"

"Three gents—Cullen Brozlin, the prez of Gunsmiths, Dennis Barragray, the veep, and Vincent Temmerson, the treasurer of the Technical Employees Union."

"And nobody else can touch the money?"

Dillinger shrugged. "Not directly, but who can say who one of those three is likely to pass it on to."

"All three of them don't have to be in on a withdrawal?"

"Naw, any one of them can take out whatever he wants."

"Is the twenty five million still there?"

"Was the last time I looked."

Jake said, "All right, Dillinger, now let's get back to the other end. You implied that the money didn't originate with the Zabicas Cartel over in Madrid?"

Dillinger had been working on the keys as Jake talked. He glanced up now, frowning. "What do you know?"

"Something wrong?"

"I've been trying to go back to the point I was at when I poked into this before. Trying to get back to the source of the loot, you know," explained the android. "But this is getting odd. Somebody's put up extra blocks since last time I was browsing, and it looks like maybe I was wrong about the original source. Hey, they're trying to—trying to—"

A small flash of intense blue light grew out of the small

computer screen. It seemed to swallow up the android's right hand and then go sizzling up his arm.

He made a surprised, whimpering sound and stood straight up. His small computer fell, hit a gnome and then bounced to the gritty earth. His straw hat popped free of his head and his arms went, rigid, to his sides.

Dillinger tried to speak, but no words came out. He stood stiff as a soldier at attention and he began gnashing his teeth. Then silence filled him and he fell over with a rattling crash.

The fallen computer spoke. "Don't follow this any further, Cardigan," it warned. Then it, too, died.

11

The Emergency Center in the Santa Monica Sector was down near the Pacific Ocean. The visitor parking/landing area overlooked a wide stretch of yellow beach and the clear blue sea. When the black skycar descended for a landing, ten seagulls had been waddling over the grey surface of the field. They scattered now, swirling up into the afternoon.

The man who stepped out of the car was lean, deeply tanned and wearing a dark blue suit. He reached back into the car, poking around in a scatter of ID badges that were strewn on the passenger seat. Selecting one that identified him as Dr. Warren S. Heddison of the Woodland Hills Sector, he attached it to his jacket.

The badge was completely convincing and in less than

five minutes he was on Level 13 and striding toward Jabb
Marx's room.

A white enameled medibot was placing a lunch tray on
the stand beside the banged-up detective. "Good afternoon, doctor."

"That'll be all for now, nurse. I'm this man's medgroup
physician and I have to do a prelim."

"As you wish, doctor."

When the bot was gone, the tanned man moved closer
to the bed. "Broken nose, three cracked ribs, minor con-
cussion," he said slowly. "I am mightily impressed, Jabb."

The big operative said, "Listen, he's a dirty fighter.
Hell, he kneed me in the balls before I even—"

"We hired you, old man, because of your reputation
for being a dirty fighter," reminded the spurious doctor.
"We wanted somebody inside the Kendricks agency
who'd be able to pick a fight with Cardigan and incapacitate him."

"Soon as I get out of here, I can—"

"No, you won't make any further attempts, Jabb." He
shook his head.

"But, listen, about the fee you promised. I really need
the money, what with two ex-wives and a kid who—"

"Oh, we always pay, regardless of results. That's agency
policy." He went over to the window. "Damn, a gull
just crapped on my car."

"I know I can take care of Cardigan if you give me—"

"We'll use some other plan." He smiled as he turned
to face the injured detective. "How does this sound? We
have you beaten up so severely that you die. Then we see

that Cardigan is framed for the job. That would get him off the Devlin Gun business, wouldn't it?"

"That's not funny."

"Have I ever claimed to be a comedian?" he asked. "No, I'm a very effective government agent. And that, I assure you, is a job where a sense of humor is a distinct handicap."

"Quit talking about having me killed, funny or not."

The false Dr. Heddison said, "I really dropped in to tell you that you're to be paid, despite the way you futzed up the job. In fact, the ten thousand dollars has already been, discreetly, deposited in your various accounts."

"Great, I really appreciate—"

"But, old man, you have to be extremely careful from here on out. Don't confide in anyone, don't go near Cardigan again. Is that understood?"

"Listen, in spite of the thing with Cardigan going wrong—I'm still a pro. I'm not going to screw up again, Gardner."

"Ah, but you just have." He frowned in disappointment. "You used my name."

"Nobody's here and the room isn't tapped. I checked that."

"So did I. Yet it's bad policy, Jabb, to use my name at all."

"Hell, I'm not even certain your name is Gardner Munsey. So even if—"

"I'll be going now," he announced. "Enjoy your lunch and watch yourself." He walked to the door. "We'll be watching you, too."

WOLFE BOSCO SIGHED a large forlorn sigh. "I'm ashamed to have you see me like this," said the small, wrinkled man, both elbows resting on top of his narrow little desk.

Jake was sitting opposite him in one of the many small cubicles on this level of the Actors Guild:America offices in the Hollywood Sector of Greater LA. "I've seen you somewhere before—in a more elevated occupation?"

Bosco sat up and spread his arms wide. "It's me, Jake. Wolfe Bosco, once a crackerjack talent agent, here and then up on the New Hollywood satellite. At present, alas, a mere shadow of my former grand self."

"That's right, you've helped us with information on a couple cases," recalled Jake. "Up on that movie satellite a few months ago you provided Gomez with—"

"That guy." The little fallen agent made a wry face. "I was living like a king, my client Jacko Fuller was starring in *Love Me Forever* and then—"

"He's an android, isn't he? You must be a great agent to con them into hiring an andy and thinking he's not."

"Like I told your Judas of a partner, Jake, everybody in the movie business is young, extremely youthful," he said. "They didn't know that my Jacko was merely a replica of a big superstar of a generation ago. Hell, they didn't even tumble to the fact he isn't flesh and blood," he said sadly. "Not until Gomez goes and spills the beans."

"Nope, Wolfe. Gomez didn't tell anybody about your con."

"You think not? Well, it was just one day—" He held up a single, knobby little finger. "One day after him and that skinny carrot-topped Newz reporter scrammed off New Hollywood, I was called on the carpet by the adolescent who was producing this epic flicker. Me and Jacko got bounced right then and there and it's been downhill ever since." He raised a hand and let it fall, rapidly, to smack the desktop. "We're rooming in a dump on LaCienega that's even rattier than the place we shared before we ascended to fame and fortune."

Jake said, "If you're finished with the autobiography, Wolfe, I'd like to commence with the business I came here for."

"You want to hire some talent?" He eyed Jake hopefully. "I still run a little agency on the side and maybe I got somebody to fill the bill." He lowered his voice. "Strictly speaking, I'm not supposed to do this, but for an old friend and customer—"

"I'm trying to locate a young woman who figures in a case we're working on, Wolfe," Jake told him, taking a sheet of faxpaper out of his coat pocket. "Here's my search permit from the front office."

"This is going to be dull," lamented the little agent. "It isn't even show business."

"I think maybe she's an actress. Called herself Janine Traynor, but there's nobody by that name living or working in Greater LA," said Jake. "I'll give you a description and we can see if it fits anybody in the Guild files."

"Okay, okay." With no enthusiasm whatsoever, Bosco pulled a keypad over closer to the center of his desk. "A few months ago I was basking in the perennial sunshine up on New Hollywood. Today, boy, I'm helping a seedy skip tracer track down some fleabrained actress. That's what they call tragedy, Jake—a fall from greatness."

"Sad," said Jake. "Are you ready?"

"Yeah, in a sec." He hit a key and behind him a large rectangular wall panel changed into a vidscreen. "Commence with the description of this strayed lady."

On the screen appeared a woman's face.

"We'll start with the hair," said Jake. "It was dark and—"

"Hold your horses." Bosco pushed at another key and another panel blossomed into a screen. It showed forty eight squares, each a different dark shade. There was a number superimposed on each. "We go about this scientifically around here. Which kind of dark hair are we talking about?"

After studying the chart for a moment, Jake replied, "Number thirty."

The woman in the picture acquired dark hair of shade #30.

In a little over ten minutes there was a photo of the woman who told Jake she was Janine Traynor on the wall behind the little agent.

"That's her," decided Jake. "Is she in your files?"

"If she's an actress, she's got to be." He, boredom showing on his wrinkled little face, poked at another key.

A small box appeared at the bottom of the photo of Janine. It read—*No person of this description on roster.*

Jake said, "Tell them to look for her with different color hair."

"More dull work."

Janine turned to a redhaired young woman in the picture. A new box announced—*Janet Mavity/Guild Card #137596-SS/ Rep: Self.*

"Address?" requested Jake.

Bosco flicked a toggle at the edge of his desk and a faxmemo came fluttering up out of a slot. "What do you know?—she lives in the Sherman Oaks Sector. That's a high-rent part of town—especially for a gal who doesn't even have an agent."

Grinning, Jake took the memo. "Much obliged, Wolfe." He got up. "Good luck to you and Jacko."

"If this redhead kid doesn't work out for you, Jake," said Bosco as Jake took his leave, "I represent at least three dames who are ringers for her and sexier."

12

The pretty blonde android took Gomez by the arm. "If you'll come with me, *por favor*," she requested.

"You speak a little Spanish I see." He accompanied her toward an arched doorway at the far end of the huge, windowless Reception Room RD#2.

"I'm the latest model Mechanix International Customer Services android," she explained, smiling politely. "Functioning as such in any part of California requires being able to communicate in Spanish."

"*Sí*, I should have realized," said the detective. "I thought the initial sight of my Latino charm had given you the gift of tongues."

"You're *muy loco*, Mr. Gomez." She led him into a lengthy corridor with plastiglass walls. "I mean that in a positive sense, of course."

The walls were illuminated and filled with pale blue water. Hundreds of small, bright tropical fish flickered and flashed within the walls.

"Nice aquarium," he observed.

"Mr. Barragray collects fish."

"Obviously."

At the back door at corridor's end, she stopped. "It's been nice meeting you, Mr. Gomez," she assured him. *"Vaya con dios."*

"Gracias."

She let go his arm, turned and walked back the way they'd come.

The door whispered open. Another pretty android, this one dark-haired, stood smiling just across the threshold. *"Como esta?"* she asked, smiling. "If you'll come along with me, I'll escort you to Mr. Barragray's private office."

"More fish," he noticed.

The high plastiglass walls of this new corridor were also full of tiny flashing fish.

His android guide slowed, pointing. "Look! The little purple one just ate a silver one," she said. "I find that amusing."

"They built in a sense of humor along with your lin-guistic abilities."

Barragray was a tall, broadshouldered man in his early forties. His blond hair was wavy and long and he had a checkered cloth napkin tied around his thick neck. "*Bue-*

nas dias, Mr. Gomez," he said, standing up behind his low wide lucite desk.

"I see they programmed you, too."

"How's that?"

"Nothing, a little android humor."

"I'm human, I assure you, although some of the staff think I've got gears inside me instead of organs." He gestured at a chair and sat down again. "I was having a little lunch. Too busy to get out today. Join me?"

"No, thanks."

"We have an excellent galley on this floor, I saw to that. I can have them send in some enchiladas or tamales."

"Actually, I eat only Hungarian food." He settled into the indicated chair.

"How's that? Oh, I see—more humor."

Gomez smiled, then asked, "You and Peter Traynor were friends?"

Barragray set down the fork he'd picked up. "I certainly tried to be Pete's friend," he answered. "As I'm sure you know already, Amy St. Mars and I have been good friends since college days over in Europe. Pete, though—I made a real effort to get close to the guy, but without much luck, I'm afraid."

"You were aware he was addicted to Tek?"

"Yes, it was obvious." He paused to eat some of his brown rice. "There are, I'm afraid, a few other employees in this division who use the stuff regularly. But if they do their work—most of them are exceptionally bright, by the way—it's my policy to let them stay on." He set the fork to one side again and leaned back in his chair. "Pete had just about reached, I have to admit, the limits of toleration around here. I was trying to stay on his side and keep him on our payroll—he was a very gifted technician in spite of his habit—but I've been under increasing pressure of late to sever him." He looked directly at Gomez. "There's no possibility, I suppose, that his death was a suicide?"

"None. Why?"

"Pete had been getting worse lately. Jumpy, depressed, suspicious," said the Gunsmiths, Ltd., First Vice President. "You've heard, I'm sure, of his completely unfounded suspicions about weapons being smuggled out of our San Andreas Arsenal facility?"

"*Sí.* Unfounded, huh?"

Barragray ate again. Eventually he said, "There is absolutely nothing going on at Gunsmiths—at any of our locations—that I don't know about. That's why I've been able to keep the position of First Vice President of the whole organization for over five years. And, I might add, why I'll be President when Cullen Brozlin decides to step down." He took up the fork and pointed it at the detective. "No, Mr. Gomez, if there were anything missing from the warehouse there, I'd be fully aware of it."

"Did you go there and check?"

"Of course. Even though all our people there and the computers confirmed there had been no thefts of any sort." He spread his hands wide. "There is nothing— *nada,* Mr. Gomez—that is missing."

"Not even a batch of the Devlin Guns?"

"Not even one of them."

Gomez rubbed at his moustache. "What exactly is the Devlin Gun?"

"A remarkable weapon. A pity it was outlawed." He dropped the fork, undid the napkin and left his desk.

There was a large holo platform in front of the left-hand wall of his large office.

Crouching, Barragray punched out something on a keypad at the edge of the platform. "This is a demo we produced some years ago," he explained. "At the time, of course, we had no idea that the UN was going to be so conservative about the Devlin Gun and forbid its use." He chuckled. "A lot of them, the UN people, nicknamed it the Devil Gun."

A field of grass came to bright life on the platform. Standing in the knee-high grass was a young man wearing only a pair of shorts. He was about two feet high.

"Oh, keep in mind that this is all simulation stuff, no matter how real it looks," said Barragray. "We don't, despite what our critics think, ever test our weapons on human guinea pigs."

A second figure appeared, wearing a camouflage suit. She was holding an odd ivory-colored gun with a stubby barrel in her right hand.

"You'll find this quite interesting," predicted Barragray. Squatting on his heels, he watched the stage intently.

The young man had seen the woman soldier and he started to run from her.

Slowly, she raised the gun. She aimed and squeezed the trigger.

There was no sound, no projectile, no beam.

But all at once the running man began to collapse in on himself. His legs turned to flabby sacks of flesh and crumpled. His torso seemed to lose its skeletal structure and cave in. In less than sixty seconds there was only a sprawled sack of wrinkled skin spread across the grass. Blood and innards and yellow fluid were leaking out of it.

Gomez gave up his chair, turned his back on the holostage and walked away from it. "Quite a demonstration."

"What the Devlin Gun accomplished is simple," said Barragray to his back. "It disintegrates the bones of the body, all of them and very swiftly. You might say it causes a sort of incredibly accelerated form of osteoporosis. Without any skeleton inside, the body becomes, to put it bluntly, a sack of guts, Mr. Gomez."

"This is a wonderful business you folks run here."

"There'll always be wars and a need for new, improved weapons," Barragray informed him. "The side with the superior weapons wins. The Devlin Gun, in my opinion, is an excellent weapon. Recommended, because of its relatively short range, for guerrilla and commando operations."

"And not one of those guns is missing?"

"As I've already assured you. I personally made certain of that."

"What do you think gave Traynor the idea that a sizable quantity of the damned things had been stolen?"

Barragray tapped the side of his head and smiled sadly. "Tek," he answered. "As I understand it, sometimes the hallucinations continue even after you unhook from the Brainbox. And, let me add, Mr. Gomez, even though I thought Peter Traynor was imagining things—I did make a very thorough, and personal, investigation of his allegations."

"If nothing's wrong at Gunsmiths and Traynor hadn't stumbled onto any hijacking—why do you think he was killed?"

Barragray moved behind his desk again. "Tek," he replied. "The whole trade is controlled by criminals."

"Traynor annoyed somebody in the Tek business and they had him killed, huh?"

"That's about it, yes. He aroused someone's ire and he suffered the consequences. Whatever is behind his death, it has absolutely nothing to do with Gunsmiths, Ltd."

"Well, that's all for now. I appreciate your help," said Gomez. "Now, if you'll summon one of those Spanish-speaking andies to guide me out of here, I'll bid you adíos."

13

Jake repeated, "Landing permission requested."

In response the fuzzy squawking noise came again out of the voxbox on the dash of his skycar.

It was late afternoon and he was circling the grounds of the large Sherman Oaks Sector home where the actress Janet Mavity was supposed to live. Next to the neoredwood and plastiglass house was a small landing area.

Twice now Jake, having noticed the red secsystem box next to the landing square, had asked to be cleared to set down.

After the second series of static-filled squawks, he said aloud, "Must be on the fritz."

He tapped out a landing pattern and the car dropped down and landed unhindered.

First easing his stungun out of its shoulder holster, Jake stepped out in to the hazy afternoon.

Suddenly from his right came a sputtering, popping sound. Bringing up the gun, he spun, in time to see the high thick hedge of hydrangeas vanish. Only the long narrow holoplatform remained.

Then, a few yards beyond the landing square, a decorative sundial began to flicker. It vanished completely in about fifteen seconds.

Alert, gun ready, Jake, cautiously, approached the house.

A side door stood open. Immediately inside a body lay, facedown, in the shadowy corridor.

Carefully, Jake moved to it. "Android butler," he realized while kneeling down next to it.

Someone had used a heavy instrument on the mechanical man's skull. It was dented, broken open in two places. Curls of colored wire and tiny plastiglass tubes had spilled out onto the plaztiles, along with a growing pool of thin ocean-blue lubricant.

The big house was silent, and as Jake walked farther along the corridor the silence closed in around him.

He found another dead android, a maid this time, sprawled in the highdomed living room. Otherwise, though, everything was in place. No furniture was overturned, not a single holovase had been knocked to the thermorug.

The entire house was like that, all in order. Except for the central control computer on the basement level. There the entire house management and security system had been shut down. But unobtrusively and deftly, so that no alarm was given and no backup system took over.

There was one other unusual thing about the dead house. Jake couldn't find a trace of anyone's having lived there. No personal effects at all. In one of the three second-level bedrooms he thought he noticed a faint trace of floral perfume, a scent he vaguely associated with the woman who'd told him she was Traynor's sister.

"That's not evidence of a damn thing," he told himself.

He made another slow circuit of the room, but there was nothing at all to be found.

When he looked toward the doorway, he saw a thin young man, not quite twenty, standing timidly there and smiling at him. "I followed you here, Jake," he explained in a mild, quiet voice. "I hope you don't mind." He held a battered black briefcase pressed close to his narrow chest.

"Depends on who you are." He still had his stungun in his hand.

"Well, you don't know my name. I've been careful about that." The young man took a step into the bedroom. "After what happened today, though—I'm darned scared, Jake. They're going to kill me next."

"And what happened today?"

"You don't need that gun, Jake," the young man told him. "You and I have worked together a lot over the past few years, but you never knew what I looked like. I'm Frank Bannett, Jr."

"Don't know you."

"That's right, you were saying that just today out in the Palm Springs Sector." He slid a hand inside the brief-case. "I'm the one who built Dillinger. We just did that tracing of Wes Flanders's activities for you."

"Oh, I see, yeah."

"But this is getting too dangerous. They destroyed Dillinger and I'm afraid I'm next." The young man came closer. "Here, let me show you something." His hand went deeper into the briefcase.

Jake grinned at him. He swung the stungun up and shot him square in the head.

14

She was slim and pretty and her hair was a glowing golden blonde. Wearing a black skirtsuit, she was standing in the exact center of the highdomed living room, a glass of white wine in her left hand. "You're home early, darling," she said.

All up above the clear oneway plastiglass ceiling of the beachside villa scores of white gulls were wheeling and turning in the oncoming dusk.

Dennis Barragray hesitated in the doorway. "I'm worried, Jean."

Jean McCrea shrugged. "You're always worried lately, darling."

He came into the room. "You've called me darling twice already."

She laughed. "And how do you interpret that?"

"I don't know," said Barragray. "It doesn't, somehow, sound like affection."

"What else could it be?"

He didn't answer immediately. Finally he asked her, "You do still like me, don't you, Jean?"

"Who wouldn't like you? The man who's in line to head Gunsmiths, Ltd." She took a small sip of her wine. "What, exactly, has put you in this lousy mood, dear?"

"Do you like this house?"

"Of course. Otherwise I wouldn't stay. I'd move out and you could spend more time with your wife."

"I want you to stay here, Jean."

"But you?"

He crossed to low white sofa but didn't sit on it. "The Cosmos Detective Agency sent a man to talk to me today."

"Did you actually talk to him. You don't, a man in your position, have to do that, do you?"

"A man, even in my position, with nothing to hide always talks to them." He frowned up at the circling gulls. "What do you suppose all those damn birds are so excited about?"

"Garbage. Which operative did you talk to?"

"Some flippant Mexican." He sat down, stood up.

"Were you hoping for Jake Cardigan?"

"What do you know about Jake Cardigan?"

"He's probably their most famous op," Jean said, rubbing the rim of the glass across her chin. "I've seen him on the vidnews lots of times."

"Well, the one I got was named Gomez."

"Cardigan's partner."

"Yes, that's right. It was all in the report our people gave me on Cosmos."

"Sit down, darling," she suggested. "We can talk this all out."

Barragray remained on his feet, watching the gliding seagulls overhead. "Killing someone, even when it doesn't go smoothly, usually doesn't bother me," he said. "But getting rid of Peter Traynor—it's not that we were especially close. And—I don't know—the way it was done."

"Not very subtle." She smiled up at him over her wineglass. "It couldn't be that at your advanced age you're developing a conscience, dear?"

"I'm not that old—not all that much older than you."

"Only twenty-some years older," said Jean, sitting on the couch and crossing her legs. "What were you referring to when you said you wanted me to stay here?"

"I'm thinking of going away for a while. Short vacation."

"Alone?"

"Yes, completely alone," he said. "And, you know, the money I've been setting aside—I might just take that along."

"In case you don't come back?"

"Oh, I'll come back. But I'd feel better with that along with me."

"It's only about—how much is it now?—a million dollars."

"Closer to two," he answered. "I can get along on that for a while if I have to."

"But I thought it was a collection," said Jean. "Paper currency from the twentieth century."

"It's a collection, but it happens to be worth nearly two million dollars."

"All the things you've done, dear, all the arms deals and the bribes and the quiet assassinations you've okayed," she said. "How come this one upsets you so?"

"I don't know." He came over and sat beside her on the low sofa. "It was while I was talking to that damned detective. I seemed to detach from everything for a minute or two. It was like dying, and it scared the hell out of me."

"A vacation will fix you up." She put her hand over his.

He moved his hand. "Your hand is cold."

"Chilled wine does that. When do you figure to go?"

"Soon. In a day or so."

"It's a good idea, darling." She leaned closer to him and kissed him, once, on the cheek.

THE ROBOT IN the shabby green tuxedo said, "You don't want the blintzes."

Gomez gave him a inquiring look. "Milt's Delicatessen is noted throughout the West for its blintzes."

"Not tonight."

"What, then?" asked the detective.

"The only thing I'd trust is the chicken soup."

Shaking his head, Gomez said, "Nope, I'm not in the

mood for that this evening. Just bring me a cup of nearcaf for now."

"A real spender I got here."

As the waiter shuffled away from the small ground-level booth, Jake arrived and slid in opposite his partner. "Have a profitable day?"

"Fairly so—and quite scary at one point. And you?"

"Memorable." Jake filled him in on his encounters with Dillinger, Wolfe Bosco and the young man who'd followed him to the Sherman Oaks Sector.

After he finished, Gomez asked, "How'd you know the lad wasn't the creator of the Dillinger andy?"

"Because, Sid, I happen to know who the true owner and operator of that Banx-tapping operation is," he replied, grinning. "I made it my business to find out quite a while ago, but I've never let on to Dillinger. Whoever sent this kid to get rid of me was obviously eavesdropping electronically on my meeting in the Palm Springs Sector today, where I kidded with the andy about being ignorant as to who was behind him."

"And this *cholo* had a lazgun in his reticule?"

Jake nodded. "Yeah, I found it in his briefcase after I stungunned the lad."

"Am I correct in assuming, *amigo*, that this assassin turned out to have no idea who actually hired him? He's a freelance murderer and was contacted anonymously, paid a fee and prepped on what to say and do."

"That's my boy, yeah," agreed Jake. "I turned him over to the SoCal cops and then ran a make on him. He works out of the San Diego Sector, has four arrests but no convictions and his name is Clare Victor Hillman."

Gomez said, *"Gracias,"* as the greenclad waiter plopped a cup of nearcaf down in front of him.

"Don't thank me until after you taste it." The waiter scowled at Jake. "You just here to try out the seating arrangements?"

"I'll have the blintzes."

"Coming right up."

Gomez tugged at the side of his moustache. "Before Dillinger became nothing more than a defunct mechanism sprawled upon the burning sands of the desert, he claimed that there was a transfer of an enormous amount of *dinero* from certain interests in Spain into the coffers of Gunsmiths, Ltd., right?"

"Into a fund that certain folks connected with Gunsmiths can access," said Jake. "Keep in mind, Sid, that we don't as yet know what the money was paid for."

"Devlin Guns would by my guess," said his partner. "Ah, and speaking of that little dingus—let me describe to you the demo I got from Barragray." He went on to tell Jake about what he'd seen on the holostage in the executive's office.

"That's a rough one," observed Jake when he'd finished. "Hate to think there are hundreds of those floating around. Particularly since they may be in the hands of the Zabicas Cartel by now."

"It's definitely kindly old Teklord Carlos Zabicas who is the recipient of the missing weapons?"

"Probably, Sid, although Dillinger—just before he ceased to be—was implying that, while Zabicas is the customer, he wasn't the original source of the money."

"If Dillinger was right—and considering that they knocked him off to keep him from giving you more colorful details, we have to conclude he was—then the trail doesn't end in Madrid."

"We've got a couple of other informants who can tap bank records," said Jake. "I'll hit one of them tomorrow. It'll more than likely turn out that newer, stronger barriers have been put up between us and the information we want—but I'll give it a try."

Gomez tried his nearcaf. "*Ai, muy malo*, says our dining-out critic," he remarked. "Barragray, by the way, assured me that nothing was missing, nobody was on the take and that the late lamented Pedro Traynor was simply one more goofy Tekkie. From what you found out, the *hombre* was lying."

"Probably so. Although it's possible that Dillinger was fed some fake information and that the Tek money never ended up with anyone connected to Gunsmiths."

"Naw, something has to be going on wrong with those Gunsmiths *pendejos*," Gomez said. "Too many people and mechanisms involved with them are biting the dust."

"That's what—Excuse me a minute." The band of his wristphone had begun contracting and expanding. "Yeah?"

"It's Dan," came the voice of his son. "I think you'd better get home—if you can."

"More trouble?"

"Not exactly, but there's someone here who's very anxious to talk to you and pass along some information."

"Who?"

"She says her name won't mean anything," answered
Dan. "But to tell you she's the one who owned and oper-
ated Dillinger."

15

Bev Kendricks said, "About time we had some lights."

The windows in her office blanked, light blossomed overhead and at floor level.

The black young woman sitting on the other side of her desk said, "You were right about Jabb Marx."

"I really wasn't sure," admitted the blonde detective. "That's why I put you on him, Katie."

"Well, Jabb is most certainly not working solely for us," said Katie McTell. "I'll give you the stuff I got on him by doing a Banx tap in a while. First off, though, *jefe*, I—"

"Where'd you pick up that *jefe*?"

"Jake's partner, Gomez. He always refers to Bascom that way."

Smiling, Bev said, "You'll pick up bad habits if you hang around with him too much."

"I certainly hope so," said Kate. "As I was saying, chief, I picked up some interesting stuff at the hospital. Look on yonder wall for a minute, will you?"

On one of the large rectangular vidscreens pictures now appeared. It was silent footage, showing the busy lobby of the Santa Monica Emergency Center. The picture froze and zoomed in on a lean, tanned man who had been heading up a ramp.

"I managed, at no cost to the expense account, to get a copy of the secsystem tapes at SMEC." Get-ting up, Katie went over to tap the image of the tan man. "This guy visited Jabb and stayed nearly fifteen minutes."

"I don't recognize the guy," said Bev.

"Fortunately, I sure do. There's some doubt as to his true name, but he's known as Gardner Munsey to the intelligence community."

Bev went over to stand beside her operative. "Munsey is somebody I've heard of," she said. "An agent of the US Office of Clandestine Operations, isn't he?"

"Right, and Munsey specializes in troubleshooting— and, sometimes, in cleaning up after operations get screwed up. Sort of the like the guy who follows the elephants in a parade with a big broom and a bucket." Katie moved a few feet back from the wallscreen. "Trouble-shooting, as defined by the OCO, includes arranging assassinations."

"So he might be involved in the death of Wes Flanders." Bev went back to her desk. "As well as Peter Traynor."

"Okay, but if that's true, what's he using Jabb Marx for?"

"To keep informed on how close we're getting to solving the Flanders case," Bev answered. "And to incapacitate Jake. They obviously want to sideline him and keep him from working on the Traynor business."

"According to the money trail, Jabb's been getting a fat government subsidy for over a month."

"Meaning the guy was recruited after we went to work on the Flanders case."

Kate sat down again and said, "I heard you chastising Jake for working Jabb over. That was an act, huh?"

"I was pretty sure Jabb had provoked Jake into a fight," answered Bev. "It's my guess he anticipated being on the winning side. Whoever's running him at the OCO wanted to stop Jake but, apparently, not kill him."

"It sure didn't work out that way for Jabb."

"No, Jake is pretty tough—and extremely competent."

"Which is why you like him."

"But Jake didn't have to be so brutal in what he did," Bev continued. "He's got an unruly temper—and he's still much too preoccupied with the death of Beth Kittridge. So, even though I was putting on an act for Jabb's benefit, some of what I said to Jake was what I really felt. Does that make sense?"

"To me," said Katie. "You're going to have to tell Jake what we've found out about the OCO's being involved."

"I will, yes," said Bev. "After I explain why I was so bitchy with him."

THE GIRL IN the wheelchair was thirteen years old. She was thin and pale and wore a dark pullover and dark slax. The chair was large and chromeplated and had obviously been expertly augmented and adapted from a standard Mechanix International model.

As Jake entered the living room of his condo, he grinned at her. "Hi, Jimmy," he said. "This is my partner, Sid Gomez."

"You're a heck of a lot smarter than I thought," Jimmy Bristol admitted to him. "How long've you known who I was?"

"Since shortly after I started using Dillinger as a source of information." Jake sat in a tin slingchair. "I like to know who's behind what I'm being told. To make sure I'm not being fed something from some Tek cartel or a rival detective agency that's bent on leading me astray."

Gomez joined Dan on the sofa. "And this *niña* is the only daughter of Joseph S. Bristol, noted plutocrat and a very highly placed vice prez of the Banx operation."

"I don't live with him any longer," said Jimmy.

"You learned a lot about the inner workings of the Banx setup before you moved in with your mother last year," said Jake.

"That's because I had a lot of time on my hands," she told him. "When you're crippled and ugly, most people don't want to have anything to do with you. Not even when you're as rich as I am."

Jake nodded at his partner. "You're a top-seeded detective, Sid. What does the evidence convey to you?"

Eyeing the ceiling, Gomez said, "Judging by the clues, I'd say we've got a bad case of self-pity, *amigo.*"

"Hey, the poor kid's not faking," said Dan, scowling at Gomez and then his father. "She really does have serious problems."

"Like everybody else." To the crippled girl Jake said, "If you're through trying to impress us with your sad lot, suppose we get to why you're here."

"I'm sorry I came." She glared at him. "I had something important to pass along to you. And, after what happened to Dillinger, I figured you were in serious danger, too." She touched a button on the chair arm and the chair started rolling for the way out.

"Stay awhile," suggested Jake.

"Why? So you can tell me what a complete mess I am?"

"We've had a lot of conversations, even if they weren't face-to-face," he reminded her. "You know what I think of you, Jimmy?"

"That I'm funny looking and—"

"That you're terrifically bright and gifted," he corrected. "Once you graduate out of this poor-little-me mode, I imagine you'll accomplish quite a lot."

"Pep talk," she muttered, thin fingers drumming on the chair arm. "Sermon."

"You might utilize your talent," added Gomez, "to do

something a mite more ennobling than dealing in boot-leg financial information, *chiquita*."

"Oh really?" She made a faint chuckling noise inside her narrow chest. "You guys both bought a lot of that bootleg info from me and Dillinger."

"That's business," said Jake. "I'll buy information from just about anybody and I don't care much about how they came by it."

"Then why make an exception with me?"

Dan said, "I think I see what he's trying to do, Miss Bristol."

"Good for you. He's your father, *you* listen to him."

"In his blunt, heavy-handed way, he's trying to get you to forget about your personal problems and concentrate on getting on with—"

"Personal problems? What kind of halfassed euphe-mism is that? I've got a defective spine and not even all the Bristol money could fix it right. It bought me a nice wheelchair, but—"

"Suppose Sid and I take a leisurely stroll along the beach?" suggested Jake. "You think you'll be in the mood to talk by the time we get back?"

Jimmy touched a button on the chair arm again. The big silvery chair started rolling for the doorway again. Then the chair halted when she was still several feet from leaving. Slowly, the metal chair did an about-face and carried her back to the center of the room again. "You really do like me, don't you?" she asked Jake in a sur-prised and perplexed tone.

"Quite a bit, yeah," he said.

"Me, too, *niña*," volunteered Gomez. "And, as one of the top-seeded experts on women in the whole state, I can assure you that you fall into the cute category."

"Latino hogwash," she said, starting to smile a little.

"Of all the brands of hogwash available at the moment," the curlyhaired detective said, "Latino is the best. Much better for you and no serious side effects."

She sighed out a slow breath. "I'll tell you something," she said to all of them. "I'm sort of scared for myself, too. They tumbled to what I was using Dillinger for and they tracked him to the hideout in the Palm Springs Sector. I was really upset when they disabled the poor guy."

"You can construct another Dillinger," said Jake.

"Sure, but it'd take months," the thin girl said. "Besides, as Gomez pointed out, it may well be time for me to move on to something else."

Jake asked her, "Do you have something else to tell me?"

She nodded her head. "After they hurt Dillinger, immediately after and before I started getting uneasy, I was just simply mad," Jimmy began. "So I used the equipment I keep at home in the Westwood Sector to do some more poking," she explained, leaning forward in the chair and gripping both the chromeplated arms. "It was very difficult, because they'd erected all sorts of new barriers." She paused, smiling with satisfaction and pride. "But, hell, I'm better at this than just about anyone."

"Even so, it's probably a good idea to quit annoying these folks for now, Jimmy."

"I probably will," she said. "Anyway, Jake, here's what I

found out. Carlos Zabicas, of the big Spanish Tek cartel, made the arrangements with Barragray to get a shipment of Devlin Guns to him in Madrid."

"*Chihuahua,*" commented Gomez.

"But the money, not all of it anyhow, didn't come from Zabicas at all, though it was all filtered through him," Jimmy continued. "The Zabicas Cartel put up just ten million dollars. The rest of the dough . . ." She paused. "The rest of the dough came from the Weber Pharmaceutical Company of New Baltimore, Maryland."

Jake said, "Who're they a front for?"

She gave an exasperated snort. "Honestly, Jake, I thought everybody knew that the OCO used the company to funnel payoff money overseas."

Gomez sat up. "So we got the Office of Clandestine Operations in on this, too?"

Jake was thoughtful. "Why is the OCO helping a Teklord acquire a substantial supply of deadly weapons?"

"Suppose, *amigo,* that Zabicas wants those nasty gadgets for somebody else?"

"Right, yeah," said Jake. "Spain is having a lot of trouble right now. President Garcia has been increasingly tough on the Tek cartels that operate in his country."

"And at least two powerful rebel terrorist groups are working to topple the prez," added Gomez. "Could our pal Zabicas be counting on the rebels, once in power, being much more cordial to the Tek trade?"

"That's got to be it."

"A nice scenario, guys," conceded Jimmy. "Trouble is, how the hell are you going to prove it all? Besides which,

I thought you two were supposed to be solving the murder of Peter Traynor?"

Jake stood up, thrust both hands deep into his trouser pockets. "It's more than likely that Barragray of Gunsmiths, Ltd., had Pete killed, using Tek goons to help him. But I doubt we can ever put together a case that'll get to court."

"There are, fortunately," said Gomez, smiling, "other ways to assure that Amy St. Mars and her offspring won't be harmed."

"Yeah, just what I've been thinking about," said Jake. "If we can throw a spanner in the works of their whole operation—expose it and get everything out in the open—then they'd have no reason to want to silence Amy."

"We'll have to move fast, though."

"I know of a way to—"

"*Ai, caramba.*"

"What's wrong?"

"The easiest way to do this is to bring my old nemesis, Natalie Dent of the Newz vidnet organization, into this at some point fairly soon," he realized. "She can help us gather facts and, when we know exactly what's going on, she'll get it onto the Newz network and tell the whole world. She'd done that for us before."

Jake grinned. "Better get in touch with Natalie and set up a meeting for early tomorrow."

Gomez made a pained face. "I keep trying to avoid that redheaded scourge and yet—"

"I think," said Dan, "that you really like her, Sid. It seems to me you protest just a little too—"

"*Por favor*, don't try to tell me that I really am fond of that woman." Groaning slightly, he made his way over to the vidphone in the corner of the room.

Jake told Jimmy, "We'll escort you home."

"Good, that'll make me feel considerably safer."

"I've already put a Cosmos team to watching your place in the Westwood Sector. One of them tagged you over here, I imagine."

Her eyes widened. "You really are smarter than I thought."

"Apparently," he conceded.

Gomez came back from the phone. "*Muy interesante.*"

"What's interesting?"

"I couldn't get through to Nat right now, because she's overseas on an assignment and is in the field at the moment," he said. "Seems she's covering a story in Madrid, Spain."

16

The bedside vidphone buzzed at a few minutes past four AM. Jake, immediately awake, sat up and said, "Yeah?"

The phonescreen activated, showing him the frowning face of Detective Lieutenant Drexler of the SoCal State Police. "I want to see you, Cardigan."

"I'm touched. How about lunch sometime next month?"

"Get off your ass and come down here to the Long Beach Sector right now," ordered the cop.

"Is this an official summons?"

"It sure as hell is."

"Where, specifically, are you?"

"I thought you might have guessed," said Drexler. "It's the hideaway that Dennis Barragray had."

"*Had?* Is he—"

"Just get the hell down here. I'm real eager to talk to you." As soon as he gave Jake the address, the phone went blank.

DREXLER TOLD THE gunmetal forensic robot, "Outside for a few minutes. Mr. Cardigan wants to view the body."

Dennis Barragray was sprawled on his back, arms spread wide and legs twisted. Someone had used a lazgun on him, up close, and his torso had been cut nearly in two. Blood and burnt cloth covered his ruined chest.

"You knew this guy, didn't you, Cardigan?"

"Never met him. Seen his picture."

"How come Gomez called on him yesterday?"

"Agency business."

"C'mon, don't be an asshole."

"You can figure it out." Jake backed away from the body. He glanced up at the starless night sky through the domed living room ceiling.

"He was Peter Traynor's boss."

"Exactly, lieutenant, and that's why Sid had to talk to him," Jake said. "If you knew it was my partner who interviewed the guy, why drag me down here instead of him?"

The black cop crossed to a Lucite coffee table to pick

the top sheet of paper from a small stack. "This isn't Barragray's official home," he said. "In fact, his wife doesn't
even know about it. No, this place was what they call a
love nest."

"And?"

"We've talked to some of the neighbors— Yeah, I have
enough balls to wake up any and all the rich bastards
who live hereabouts," he said, passing the sheet to Jake.
"Here's a comp portrait our ID bot printed up, based on
the descriptions of the lady who was sharing this place
with Barragray. Know her?"

The young woman in the simulated photo was Janine
Traynor with blonde hair. "She looks vaguely familiar,"
said Jake. "Have you identified her?"

"The name she's been using here was Jean McCrea,"
answered the policeman. "But yesterday afternoon you
stungunned a fellow in the Sherman Oaks Sector resi-
dence of a lady known as Janet Mavity." From an inside
pocket of his jacket, he took out a folded sheet of paper.
"I happened to be going over the file on that case, since
I'm awfully interested in your activities these days,
Cardigan. I had this comp shot in my skycar with me."
He held up this second simulated photograph. "Except
for the red hair, this is the same lady who was in resi-
dence here."

"Say, it might be at that."

"Who is she?"

"You've got two names, Drexler—take your pick."

"I've sent both these pictures on to ID Central in

DC. But those bastards'll take a couple of days to grind out an answer as to her true identity," he said, putting the picture away. "Why were you interested in her?"

"Had a tip she was a friend of Traynor's."

"Have you contacted her?"

"Not yet." He shook his head. "Have you?"

"We think she's left the country."

"Bound for where?"

"Spain."

Jake studied the night sky again. "Spain. Interesting country."

"C'mon. Save me some time and tell me who she really is."

"I don't really know," Jake assured him. "You think she killed Barragray?"

"Too soon to tell," answered the lieutenant. "But she used to live here and now she doesn't. She left most of her clothes and belongings behind, but took enough to indicate she was skipping."

"When did she leave?"

"She took off in a skyliner three and a half hours ago."

Jake returned to the corpse. "He's been dead at least five hours."

"Five or six."

"So she could have killed him and still caught her flight."

"She booked it at the last minute, from a phone at the twenty four-hour mall a mile from here."

Jake said, "Of course, it could be she walked in and found him dead. Got scared and ran."

"That's another possibility, sure." He walked over to an open doorway. "Here's something else for you to look at, Cardigan."

"Another body?"

"No, just a hole in the wall."

There was a neat, sooty hole, about two feet in diameter, high in the cream-colored wall behind the large oval bed. "Safe, huh?"

"Used to be," said Drexler. "The house's entire secsystem, by the way, was disabled—expertly. So blowing the safe didn't ring any bells anywhere."

"Would Jean McCrea do that?"

"To get at the safe, sure."

"If she was cozy with Barragray, she'd probably have known how to open it."

"Then to make it look like an outside job."

Jake nodded at the hole. "Any idea about the contents?"

"Go over by the bed and look at the pillow. Don't touch anything."

Lying on the pillow was an antique $50 bill. "Twentieth-century currency, isn't it?"

"Nineteen-fifties. Worth about seventy-five dollars in the present collector market."

"You figure Barragray had a safe full of that kind of cash?"

"It's an assumption I'm considering. And that would give the absent Jean McCrea a nice motive for gunning the poor bastard," replied the lieutenant. "Do you know anything about a cache of old money?"

"Not a damn thing."

Drexler eyed him. "You sure you never talked to this woman—under any of her names?"

"I didn't, no," lied Jake again.

17

Gomez said, "*Ai.*" He leaned back in the pilot seat of his skycar, which was taking him through the bright clear morning. He closed his eyes, clenched his fists and groaned. Then, getting his emotions under control, he glowered at the dash panel vidphone. "*Sí*, okay. For the good of the agency, I'll accept the call."

"What sort of pagan orgy were you involved in last night, Gomez, or, which I predicted, you recall, a long time ago, is your reckless lifestyle finally catching up with you? Well, no matter, let's get down to business and start—Did you, if you don't mind my pausing to inquire, have that many wrinkles under your bleary eyes the last time we met?"

"They appeared shortly after our last encounter, Nat."

The slender redhaired reporter, Natalie Dent, nodded. "I understand, and I'm not at all flattered, since I'm aware, having been entangled with you, in a purely workaday sense, several times in the past, alas, that you've been trying to contact me numerous times over here in Spain and I'm assuming, knowing you all too well, that you're hatching some duplicitous scheme that involves hoodwinking me in order to ensure its ultimate success."

"Twice. I phoned you merely twice."

"I have an important dinner date, strictly business, with a highplaced government official here in Madrid, Gomez. He'll be calling for me in ten minutes, unless, like a great many of the people over here, he's late," the Newz reporter told him. "So, if you can cut out your usual circumlocutions and attempts to lead me up the garden path, and get right to the nubbin of what you're trying to con me into doing for you, I'd, really and truly, appreciate it." Lowering her voice, she added, "I'm using a tap-proof phone and I assume, dimwitted as you are, that you have the sense to use one, too."

"Yes, *cara*," he assured her. "Here's what I want to chat about. Jake and I are working on a case that—"

"If you're going to go on at great length about the Peter Traynor murder, spare yourself, and me, the trouble. I already know all about that."

"*Bueno*. Now, then, *cara*, we may well want to expose certain of our upcoming findings to the public," he said.

"You've been helpful in that area in the past and it's benefited your alleged career as well as—"

"You've grown, if you'll pardon my pointing this out, since I'm doing it in an absolutely constructive manner, even more longwinded, Gomez. I wonder, and maybe you'll want to see your physician, if your already understaffed brain isn't getting even more feeble as a result of your growing older and—"

"Suppose, Nat, that in a few days we pass along some information about this case? Can you see to it that—"

"What aspect exactly are you going on about? Does this have to do with the supply of outlaw Devlin Guns that was delivered to Janeiro Martinez's rebels? I already know quite a lot about that."

"*Momentito,*" he requested. "You know for certain that the guns went to Martinez and not one of the other rebel groups in Spain?"

She smiled. "Of course, didn't you?"

"We must, Natalie, compare notes on this whole setup and then—"

"That sounds just wonderful, Gomez, since, as disrespectful and sneaky as you are, and even though you're even seedier than in former times, I do, at my innermost core, have a certain amount of grudging affection for you. And I'd be an ungrateful wretch, if anybody uses that expression anymore, which I seriously doubt, if I didn't feel a certain gratitude to you for helping me get the scoop up there on the New Hollywood satellite, which enabled me to reassume my rightful position in the media world as one of the top investigative reporters going," she said. "Anytime you're in Madrid, why, I'd love to get together. Perhaps, if you pick up the tab, we can even have lunch. I have to go now."

Gomez scowled at the blank screen. *"Caramba,"* he said as the skycar set him down on the Cosmos agency rooftop.

BASCOM SAID, "I'M glad you mentioned Spain, fellas."

"Planning to send us there?" inquired Jake.

"I am indeed." The agency head was perched on the edge of his desk with his saxophone resting across his lap.

Gomez, slouching in a lime-colored bubblechair, said, "Is the Widder Traynor going to pay for the jaunt?"

"Amy St. Mars, I'm pleased to say, is not the only well-fixed client interested in the Traynor killing."

"Are we, *jefe*, going to be working for one of your sneaky government agency chums again?"

"Actually, Sidney my boy, for a pretty powerful, although unknown to the public, committee that oversees the actions of the intelligence agencies," answered Bascom. "They want us to perform, for a tidy fee, a few simple chores for them."

Jake asked him, "Such as?"

"Firstly, they'd like you to determine how and why the OCO is apparently engaged in helping to run illicit weapons from GLA to Spain," the chief began. "Next, you're to get a list of all the main participants engaged in this caper, whatever side they're on." Setting his sax aside, he left the desk. "Oh, and it would be nice—and bring us a substantial bonus—if you lads can get the Devlin Guns, every damned one of 'em, out of rebel hands and back into a safe storage spot."

Gomez smiled at his partner. "That shouldn't take more than a couple days, do you think, *amigo?*"

"Three at the most," said Jake. "We can spend the rest of our time in Spain going to robot bullfights and learning to play the guitar."

"What was I just recently warning you guys about schoolboy buffoonery?" Bascom squatted next to a holostage. "It's bad enough when you hooligans get shirty with clients of the caliber of Amy St. Mars. But bear in mind that we've got a very serious group of people running this great land of ours and it won't do to razz 'em."

Gomez produced a rude noise.

Jake said, "Are we allowed to hire some help over in Spain? Going up against Janeiro Martinez and his bunch is going to require some assistance, Walt."

"We're, in a manner of speaking, working for the government. So spend whatever you have to." Bascom tapped the keypad of the stage. "Here's some information I rounded up from a connection at the ID Central back in Washington, DC."

An image of Janine Traynor, lifesize, materialized on the stage.

"This is what she really looks like," continued Bascom. "And her real name is Janine Kanter. She's five foot four, weighs one hundred fifteen, has black hair, hazel eyes and is twenty five years old."

"Told me twenty one."

"Just one of her many bendings of the facts," said Bascom, backing from the platform and studying the young woman. "Janine Kanter graduated from the University of NorCal's Petaluma Campus five years ago with top grades. She majored in International Political Science and had a minor in Dramatic Arts. She worked for a year in Frisco at a theater run by a group calling itself Politiks Playhouse."

"She's a darn good actress," conceded Jake. "Who's she working for now?"

Bascom shook his head. "Seems to be freelancing in the political area and nobody is sure who's backing her. She doesn't go in for terrorism or assassination—or if she does, nobody's ever caught her at it. What she's been up to openly in recent times is aiding causes that some folks consider far too liberal and radical."

"Any examples?" asked Jake.

"She helped run guns into New Brazil to aid the guerrillas who were trying to topple the Furtado dictatorship, for instance. She spent some time in the Angola backcountry with Father Wepman's Christian Commandos." Bascom bent, hitting another key and Janine was gone. "Things like that, Jake."

Jake was still looking at where her image had been. "You say there's no indication she goes in for killing?"

"Nothing on her record, not even a suspicion."

"This *mujer* sounds to me like she's an idealist, in it for what she believes and not what she can make," observed Gomez. "If her record up to now is any indication, she sure doesn't sound like somebody who'd be working for the Teklords."

"And she probably didn't kill any of the guys on our growing list of victims," said Jake. "But she sure as hell must have had something to do with those smuggled guns. Especially since she seems to have been living with Dennis Barragray for the past few months."

Gomez shifted his position in his fat chair. "As I perceive this, Barragray must've been helping to get the guns to the rebels—for a handsome fee," he said. "The lady must've wanted those guns to get to their destination, so she should have been happy about what this *cabrón* was up to. Therefore, she wouldn't have sliced him up with a lazgun."

"Unless he sold the guns to the wrong rebel faction," said Jake.

Bascom cleared his throat. "You're booked on a skyliner flight that departs for Madrid at three this very afternoon," he informed them. "I suggest that you save all further speculations until you're trotting around on Spanish soil."

18

The school day had long since ended at the SoCal State Policy Academy and the second-level corridor was empty. Outside the oneway window the misty evening showed. Dan moved rapidly along, came to the door marked *Background & ID* and tapped on it quietly.

The heavy metal door hissed open.

"Geez, you took your sweet time getting here." A robot, large, wide and copperplated, popped up out of a wicker rocker.

"It takes a while to get to the Santa Monica Sector from our place," said Dan, slipping inside the big room. "You said it was important that you talk to me, Rex. So?"

Rex/GK-30 lumbered over to the nearest wall, which

was covered, floor to ceiling, with rows of infoscreens. "I was sitting and rocking here on my toke this evening—being both the librarian and the night watchman means I got a lot of time on my hands, so to speak. Anyhow, Daniel, I got to thinking about this latest case your old man is working on."

"How'd you find out about that?"

Rex's metallic eyelids clicked a few times. "Hey, didn't Molly tell you she'd been—"

"Molly Fine's been consulting you again?"

"That Molly, yes. She wanted some material on the assorted goniffs and lowlifes connected with this opus."

Dan sighed. "No, she hasn't gotten around to mentioning that as yet."

"She's an exceptional skirt," said the robot. "Feisty, independent. Not your standard confiding-type sweetheart."

"Molly's not exactly my sweetheart."

"Applesauce," remarked Rex. "You're smitten and vice versa." He pointed a coppery forefinger at one of the midlevel screens. It flashed alive. "To while away the lonely hours, I started digging deeper into the lives and times of some of the central characters in this mishmash. When I got around to the late Dr. Garret Devlin, I encountered something interesting."

"That can't be very important, Rex. Devlin's been dead and gone for years."

Rex/GK-30 gave a rattling chuckle. "Maybe yes, maybe no, kiddo."

On the activated screen a fullface and profile shot of a pudgy, balding man of about fifty appeared side by side. "Is this Devlin?"

"Himself. Out-of-shape gink, by the looks of him. With proper exercise you can add years to your life, you flesh-and-blood types."

"You were hinting that he isn't dead? That's impossible, Rex."

The photos went away, replaced by printed copy that was slowly scrolling upward across the screen. "Here you have a dull and tedious account of the skytram crash that was supposed to have put out his lights."

"Yeah, and it says right here—" Dan tapped a line of text that was slowly climbing by. "Says a DNA scan of the burnt remains positively established that the body was that of Garret Devlin, age fifty three. So?"

"Feast your glims on the next document."

An InfoRequest sheet showed up.

"Who filed that?"

Rex's chest made a mild clang when he tapped himself with his thumb. "Me. I faked a very believable and official-looking inquiry pertaining to the SoCal Coroner's Office files on the deceased. That's where the test results on the DNA scan are supposed to be, plus a sample of the material used."

A fresh document came onto the screen.

"'No such file exists,'" read Dan. "What's that mean? They've got to have the Devlin file."

"It's possible that the stuff on Devlin got misfiled

somehow," acknowledged the robot. "But, Daniel, I sort of doubt that."

"Then somebody deliberately—"

"Dan, your condo told me you'd be here." Molly Fine came hurrying into the big Background & ID room.

"What is it?"

"My Uncle Jerry—you know, the attorney from the shady side of the family tree—just phoned me at home."

"You look very upset." He took hold of her hand.

Taking a deep breath and putting her other hand on his arm, she said, "He still has contacts with some of the sleazy people he met while doing sneaky jobs for Gunsmiths, Ltd. And—well, he heard something about your father."

"Dad? Is he in trouble?"

"That flight to Spain," said Molly, talking rapidly. "Uncle Jerry doesn't have many details, but he heard they plan to try to do something to the skyliner."

"Jesus, blow it up?"

"I don't know. What you've got to do is get in touch with him right now in flight and—"

"I'll take care of that," volunteered Rex, trotting over to the nearest vidphone. "I got pals in the International Controllers Guild and they can patch us through faster than anybody." He activated the phone. "Give me the details of his flight, Daniel."

Dan did that as he hurried to the robot's side. "Who's trying to get at my Dad, Molly?"

"We don't know for sure. But my uncle is guessing it's Teklords."

"Damn it, hurry up, Rex."

The robot turned away from the phone. "No luck," he said forlornly. "They lost all contact with the skyliner over ten minutes ago."

19

The man known as Gardner Munsey was walking along a quirky lane just off Pennsylvania Avenue with his shoulders hunched and his hands clasped behind his back. There was, as he made his way through the chill, overcast DC night, a thin, satisfied smile on his tanned face.

He continued to smile as he double-timed up the stone steps of the narrow brownstone house that was his destination.

The red realwood door opened before he reached it.

A large silverplated robot in a glossy black tuxsuit was standing in the carpeted hallway waiting for him. "Not a very pleasant evening, sir," he observed.

"On the contrary, Ramus, it's a splendid night." He turned and allowed the bot to help him out of his misted grey overcoat. "Is Mrs. Spangler about tonight?"

"Unfortunately, sir, she had to escort two of the young ladies to a client's in Chevy Chase."

"Sorry to have missed the lady."

"However, sir, Miss Marie is in her usual room and awaiting you."

"Excellent, old man." He gave the robot an appreciative pat on the arm and headed up the carpeted stairway to the second floor.

At the third door on the right he tapped three times.

"Come in," invited a youthful female voice.

"It's a pleasure to encounter you again, my dear." Munsey entered the softlit, peach-colored room and shut the door quietly behind him.

The girl reclining on the antique four-poster bed was wearing only some frilly lingerie. She was lean, blonde and no more than seventeen. "How are you tonight, Mr. Munsey?"

"Just fine, dear." He smiled at her as he walked around the bed. He pressed his hand flat against a painting of a naked young woman sitting on a rock.

A section of the bedroom wall made a very slight creaking before swinging open.

Munsey said, "Nice seeing you again, Marie," and stepped through the opening.

After the wall had swung behind him, he crossed to the single chair, an antique nineteenth-century bentwood rocker. Stopping behind the chair, he rested his right hand on its twisted back. "Can we get going, old man? I've a rather full schedule this evening."

The circular holostage a few feet in front of the chair made some low clicking sounds.

The man who materialized was about forty, short and redhaired. He was grimacing and the left sleeve of his striped shirt was rolled up to nearly the shoulder. His right hand was metal and he was touching the forefinger to his bare upper arm. "Trying out another new hand, got an injection gun built in."

The dark metal hand popped twice. The redhaired man jerked twice, gritting his teeth, in his straight metal chair.

"Very impressive, Sam." Munsey settled into the bentwood chair, causing it to rock gently a few times. "Suffering for the cause. If it were up to me, old man, I'd award you a medal."

"Screw you, Munsey," said Sam Trinity, scowling. "If I don't shoot myself full of painkiller all the time, I can't really function at all." He picked up a white glove and began working it back over the metal fingers. "I wasn't in such lousy shape, hurting all the damn time, until I had my run-in with Jake Cardigan."

"Relax and enjoy it," advised the other agent. "It gives you a lovely excuse to dope yourself up."

Trinity said, "Are you taking care of Cardigan?"

"Even as we speak."

"I don't see why we can't just kill the bastard."

"The directive I'm forced to follow states he and that whimsical sidekick of his are to be incapacitated only. My assumption is that somebody higher up the line doesn't want to risk killing a couple of Cosmos ops." Munsey smiled. "Of course, old man, we're not prevented from putting Cardigan *seriously* out of action. My people have some leeway there."

"Bastard."

"Me?"

"Cardigan, I mean." Trinity leaned suddenly forward, grinding his teeth. Yanking the glove free, he administered another shot of narcotics. "It's bad tonight."

"Maybe you ought to use it to predict the weather," Munsey suggested. "I had an uncle with a cyborg leg who could tell when it was going to—"

"Fill me in on the Cardigan deal. I'm still, keep in mind, your superior."

"For now."

"What the hell does that mean?"

"Not a thing, Sam, merely idle chitchat." Munsey smiled. "Still, with an organization as volatile as our particular branch of the OCO— Well, one never can tell."

"Have you heard something, damn it?" Trinity was pulling the glove back onto his metal hand.

"No, not at all," Munsey answered. "Quit fretting and concentrate on Cardigan. Any moment now his skyliner is going to be making an unscheduled landing. We'll take care of him then."

"We ought to dump the whole damn plane in the frigging ocean."

"That's inhumane, Sam, and against agency policy," reminded the agent. "You can always hope, however, that my people become too zealous and kill him, quite by accident."

"If I was running this operation, there wouldn't have to be any hoping about it." Trinity stood up. "Report to my office soon as you hear how it turns out."

Munsey left the rocker. "Of course, old man."

"Do you ever spend any time with Marie?"

"No more than I have to."

"She's not bad in the sack. You ought to take the time to try her."

"Thanks for the recommendation, old man, but I think I'll pass."

"Your mistake." Trinity vanished from the platform.

20

Gomez had been up in the galley of the skyliner as it sped through the increasingly dark sky high above the Atlantic. "But I'm sincere, *chiquita*," he was telling the pretty blonde android attendant who was in charge of the nearcaf machine.

"You really do think so?"

"Absolutely. You're completely believable," he assured her.

She wrinkled her slightly upturned nose. "Oh, I just don't think so," she said. "I'm cute and all, but anybody can tell I'm an andy, just a dumb old machine."

"Not at all," the detective assured her. "You had me completely fooled. I mentioned to my associate earlier in the journey that it was interesting to note that the

Quixote Air Service was using human attendants instead of—"

"He's very attractive."

"Why are you talking about me in the third person, *cara?*"

"Not you, Mr. Gomez, although you're sort of okay looking in an odd sort of way. I mean your handsome friend, Mr. Cardigan." She filled another plazcup with nearcaf. "He's my idea of a really impressive man. He's obviously led a rough life, but he's still—"

"Hey, that's just a reaction they built into you, Suzi," cut in Gomez. "If you ever want to be taken for a real human being, you've got to go beyond these traditional judgments. When you can honestly appreciate an offbeat charm such as mine, then you'll be a real person inside."

"Have you known Mr. Cardigan long?"

"Since before you were built, but we're straying from the topic."

"Oh, don't be offended. It's . . ."

He waited, eyeing her. "It's what?"

Suzi stiffened, arms dropping to her side. Her eyes went wide before they both clicked shut.

Gomez shook her by both arms. "Snap out of it."

But the pretty android had ceased to function and already her very believable flesh had started to cool.

Shaking his head, frowning, he hurried across the small gallery and into the passway that led to the cabins.

A few feet ahead a male attendant was standing rigidly against a wall, eyes closed.

"*Muy malo.*" Gomez started to run.

Jake came out of their cabin before Gomez reached it, having slid the door open with his hands. "Something's wrong, Sid," he said. "Just about everything except the aircirc system has shut down in there."

"At least two of the flight andies are defunct, too." He gestured at the frozen attendant.

Someone started banging on the door of the cabin across the corridor. "My lights have gone out and my door's stuck," cried an elderly woman.

Jake crossed, prying her door open. "Some kind of emergency, ma'am."

"We're going to crash?" she exclaimed. "You can feel this plane losing altitude."

"Now that she mentions it, *amigo*, we are dropping."

Jane started moving toward the front of the skyliner. "Better talk to the pilot."

More passengers were shouting and crying out. Some of them managed to force their doors open and were spilling into the long grey corridor.

"Mostly ocean down below, if I recall my geography," remarked Gomez as he followed Jake.

"We ought to be over the Azore Islands about now."

"Not much chance of hitting one of those dinky islands when you're plummeting toward the deep blue sea."

"We're not exactly plummeting. This feels more like a descent."

"Descent or plummet, I expect to be mighty soggy any minute."

Jake knocked on the door to the pilot cabin.

There was no response.

He tugged the door aside with both hands.

The greyhaired woman in the pilot seat was absorbed with the control panel, tapping keys, twisting knobs, even whacking a dial with her clenched fist now and then. "No time for conversation, folks," she said without turning around.

"What the hell is going on?" Jake stepped into the small cabin.

"Feel like something's taken over the control of the ship," the pilot told him. "But that's not possible. All of Quixote's systems are tamper-proof. So this can't be a parasite box or—"

"According to this course screen," said Jake, tapping the oval panel, "we're scheduled to land on one of the Azore Islands."

"I know, but I had nothing to do with that," she assured him. "I can't, though, get the ship to respond at all. Somebody else is flying it."

"Looks like we'll set down in less than six minutes."

"*Amigo*, you've often heard me lecture on the scarcity of coincidences in the universe."

"I agree, Sid. This has to have something to do with us."

"*Sí*, meaning we can expect some sort of unpleasant reception down there."

"Yeah," said Jake. "And we've got about five minutes to get ready for that."

Dan said, "That's not possible, is it?"

Rex/GK-30 spread his metal hands wide. "Kids, I've checked with everybody I can think of, including a bosom buddy up in the International Flight Monitoring satellite," said the robot. "Nobody can find a trace of the Quixote skyliner carrying your pop and his partner."

"But it has to show up on the satellite scans."

"Not necessarily," said Molly, who was holding Dan's hand. "If the people who are behind this are sufficiently clever, there are several electronic tricks they can rig—all of them illegal *and* expensive. But neither of those things is a block to the Teklords."

Dan said, "We've got to talk with your uncle, Molly. See if he knows anything else about this."

"That's not going to be especially easy." She made a perturbed face. "He phoned me from Mexico and didn't bother to give me his number or mention where exactly he was."

"I can track him down," offered the robot.

"You better do that." Dan let go of Molly and hurried over to another vidphone. "I'm going to talk to Bascom if I can."

The agency head was still in his office. "I already heard, Dan," he said before the young man had finished speaking.

"So what do you know about Dad? Did they crash or—"

"We're not sure." Bascom was sitting behind his desk, leaning forward. "My guess, however, is that the crate was hijacked in some pretty sophisticated way. If it had simply crashed in the ocean, we'd know about it by now."

"The Teklords are involved in this," said Dan, explaining about what Molly's shady uncle had told her.

"They're involved in much of what befalls your father," said Bascom. "There may also be a government angle, which I'm pursuing with some of my intelligence contacts."

"You mean maybe the Office of Clandestine Operations is in on this, too? They've never liked Dad or—"

"Too soon to tell. Keep in mind that Jake and Gomez are damned good at taking care of themselves."

"Sure, but—"

"I'll call you soon as I find out anything." The screen blanked.

Rex announced, "Hot dog, I've located Jerrold Fine in the Borderland area."

Molly brightened. "Let me call him, then," she said.

21

They stood at the edge of the clearing, watching the Quixote skyliner being brought down through the warm night. Rising up behind the three figures was the immense plastiglass dome that covered the Fayal Fruit Company's #3 banana plantation.

The small field's landing lights splashed streaks of yellow across the darkclad watchers, two men and a woman.

The tallest of the trio, a lanky black man in his middle thirties, was arguing with the woman.

She was small, a shade over five feet, and wore her dark hair long. "I'm not going to do that, Charlie, no."

"I'm afraid, Almita, you're going to have to," said Charlie Lunden, holding out his hand to her. "No lazguns allowed on this mission, so give it to me."

"No lazguns for you OCO buttwipes," she said, shaking her head, angry, and backing away from the agent. "But I don't have a damn thing to do with your agency or your halfass government."

"Carlos Zabicas guaranteed your good behavior, which is the only reason you were allowed along," reminded Lunden. "Now, quick, the ship is setting down. We've got to get aboard right now and take Cardigan and Gomez."

"They're both rough bastards," insisted Almita Santos. "I'm not giving up my gun."

"Almita, dear," said the other OCO agent, a tall, husky blond man, "this is a stungun you feel in your pretty little back. Take out your lazgun, drop it. That will be more than enough crap for tonight."

"Listen, Helton, Carlos won't like you—"

"It would be a shame," said Bayard Helton, jabbing the gun barrel into her spine, "if you were seriously incapacitated—perhaps permanently—during this operation. We can blame it on Cardigan and—"

"Okay, *cabrón*." She tossed the lazgun toward the brush and the night swallowed it up.

"Cardigan and his partner are in Cabin 14," said Lunden. "But they'll be expecting trouble. Come on, let's go."

"Try to keep in mind, dear," said Lunden, prodding her with the gun, "that we're a team."

JERROLD FINE TOLD everybody he was forty seven, but shaving that six years off his age hadn't improved his appearance any. He had a sallow, deeply wrinkled face and his eyes were dull and deeply sunk. Very carefully, he ducked into the phone booth in the lobby of the Hotel Borderland. "This is Jerrold Fine," he said, almost in a whisper. "There's a personal call for me from GLA."

"What's that, *señor?*" A ball-headed gunmetal robot had shown up on the screen. "I can't hear you at all clearly."

"First—are you absolutely certain this damned vidphone is tap-proof?"

"Of course, *señor.*"

"Some of these backward Borderland setups claim they're absolutely bugfree and then it turns out—"

"I assure you, *señor,* that no one can eavesdrop on your conversation. Not even myself."

"I'm Jerrold Fine," he repeated his name in a louder voice. "There's a call from Greater Los Angeles waiting for me."

"*Sí,* from Molly Fine. *Un momento.*"

Molly showed up on the screen, replacing the bot. "Uncle Jerry, you've got to help us find—"

"Hold on just a minute, pet," cautioned her uncle as he scanned the hotel lobby through the oneway plastiglass side of the booth. "Are you completely certain you're on a tap-proof phone on your end?"

"Of course, I'm calling from the academy."

"The SoCal State Policy Academy, you mean? Oh, I don't know if I want to—"

"Please, calm down, Uncle Jerry. This is darned important to—"

"Explain who that is standing immediately behind you."

"Dan Cardigan. Dan, my uncle."

"Good evening, sir."

"Jake Cardigan's boy? Oh, I don't know about this, honey. Having direct contact with—"

"You're having direct contact with *me*," his niece told him. "Now, about that warning you gave me about—"

"I shouldn't have done that." He shook his head. "That's the trouble with still having a vestige of conscience."

"Something *has* happened to the skyliner Jake and his partner were traveling on," she said. "Do you know any more details, Uncle Jerry—more than you told me?"

"I told you too much as it was, pet. These people don't like informers."

"What people?" asked Dan.

"I don't want to be seen talking directly to Cardigan's kid."

"Tell me, then, darn it. Who, specifically, rigged this?"

"A very powerful Tek cartel, for one."

"Zabicas?" asked Dan.

After a few seconds of waiting, Molly asked, "Uncle Jerry, is it the Carlos Zabicas cartel in Madrid?"

"So I've heard."

"Who else?"

Fine studied the lobby again, watched a robot bellhop in a bright serape go hurrying up a ramp. "There's an element inside the OCO—a rogue group that doesn't always toe the line when it comes to official policy," he said. "They have had something to do with this as well."

"What exactly did they do?"

"Molly, I told you to suggest to Cardigan that he didn't take that flight. You—"

"It was too late to stop him. You have to tell me what's happened to the Quixote skyliner."

"This is all very dangerous, pet. The more I tell you, the—"

"Did it crash?" asked Dan anxiously. "Did they destroy the skyliner?"

"Tell him," said Molly's uncle, growing increasingly uneasy, "that they weren't planning, based on the limited information I have, to destroy the ship or cause it any serious damage."

Molly asked him, "What then?"

"A forced landing is what was planned. They've got some very powerful equipment, outlaw stuff, that's powerful enough to take over the control of the skyliner from a distance," explained Uncle Jerry.

"Where," asked his niece, "did they plan to land it?"

"I don't know, pet," he said. "My guess would be an island. There are a lot of the damned things scattered all across the Atlantic."

"Can you—"

"Who the hell are you?"

The door of the booth had been yanked open and a hand holding a gun thrust in.

"Uncle Jerry?"

"Goodbye, pet," he said quietly.

22

Lunden gestured again with his stungun. "It's not our intention to hurt any of you," he announced. "As soon as our routine search is complete, your skyliner will—"

"What the hell kind of routine search do you call this?" demanded a large, heavyset passenger who was standing, scowling, in the doorway of Cabin 11. "You force our damned ship down on this uncivilized island and—"

"The sooner we complete our business," said Helton, "the sooner you'll all continue on your way."

The pair of Office of Clandestine Operations agents had lined up all the 1st Class passengers—there were nine of them in the corridor. There was also still a frozen Quixote attendant standing stiffly there. Almita had gone on to explore another section of the downed skyliner.

"We're interested in the two men who were in Cabin 14," continued Lunden, "We have to know where they are."

The other agent jabbed his stungun into the drooping midsection of the belligerent man in 11. "You must know where they went," he said.

"How would I know a goddamn thing? I was stuck in this cabin until you bastards busted in."

Moving down the corridor, Lunden stopped in front of an elderly woman. "You seem awfully agitated, ma'am."

"Who wouldn't be?" she said. "This has been an outrageous—"

"Hold on, now." The black OCO agent put a hand on her thin shoulder. "Look at me, ma'am, if you would. Now tell me you have no idea where either of those men is."

"I don't," she insisted. But her eyes swung inadvertently to her left.

"The andy," realized Lunden. He shoved her back against the wall and swung his stungun up.

Gomez, who'd been standing there in the android's uniform, unfroze and dived for the floor. As he dropped, he yanked out his own stungun.

He and Lunden fired at just about the same instant.

ALMITA SANTOS PUSHED at the luggage compartment door with the hand that wasn't holding the stungun. The metal door swung open inward and remained that way.

She stood, listening, on the threshold for roughly twenty seconds before crossing into the dimlit room.

Atop the nearest stack of baggage was a white cat in a plastiglass carrying case. It began a mournful meowing the moment the young woman entered.

"Shut up, *gatito*," she suggested.

The cat ignored the request, wailing louder and clawing at the side of its container.

"*Pendejo!*" She fired the stungun and its beam struck the wailing animal.

The cat dropped, suddenly stiff, to the floor of the plastiglass case.

"If you're through playing with that gun, miss, I'd like you to toss it on the floor." Jake had stepped out from behind the open door and had his stungun touching the small, dark young woman's back.

She, muttering, dropped her weapon. "Which one are you?"

"How many others are there?" Jake asked.

"You must be Cardigan. From what I hear of Gomez, he isn't smart enough to get the drop on me."

"How many?"

"You go find out, *cabrón*. Almita moved her right hand to her left side, as though she was about to scratch herself.

Jake chopped at her wrist with the side of his hand. "I'm the smart one, remember?" He tugged the small lazgun out of the pocket she'd been aiming for.

"They didn't want me to bring a lazgun with me," she said disdainfully.

"So we're dealing with humane highjackers, huh?"

"Humane assholes. If I had my way, we—"

"Congratulations, Mr. Cardigan. I see you've been successful."

"Thus far," he said as the greyhaired woman who was the pilot of the skyliner stepped into the baggage room. "How come nobody's nabbed you yet?"

"Probably," she said as she, smiling, pointed a lazgun at him, "because I'm on their side."

GOMEZ HAD BEEN a few seconds faster. The beam of his stungun hit Lunden square in the chest, causing the OCO agent to go staggering back. The stungun shot he'd aimed at the detective went wild, just missing the elderly woman.

She started screaming.

Lunden toppled over sideways and lay, stiff, on the corridor floor.

Helton, meantime, had gone diving through the open doorway of Cabin 14.

The heavyset, angry passenger called to Gomez, "The other son of a bitch is in your old cabin, buddy."

"*Gracias.*" Gomez, watchful, got to his feet. He pried the weapon from Lunden's stiff fingers and thrust it into a side pocket of the borrowed uniform. "You all right, *señora?*"

"Not at all, young man. But I wasn't hit by any stray shots, if that's what you mean."

Nodding, Gomez called out, "Hey, *hombre*, we've got

us a standoff here. Suppose you chuck your gun out into—"

"To hell with you, Gomez," answered the OCO man from within the cabin.

"By now my partner has taken care of the feisty *señorita*," said Gomez as he inched closer to the doorway of 14. "So you're going to be alone in . . . *Si*, here they come now."

Jake had entered the corridor, followed by Almita and the pilot. "This isn't a victory parade, Sid."

Frowning, his partner inquired, "*Que pase?*"

"Well, it turns out our pilot is in cahoots with them."

The heavyset passenger complained, "Damn, this gets worse and worse. You can be damned sure Quixote is going to hear about—"

"Be quiet," ordered the greyhaired pilot, "or you'll be in no position to complain about anything."

"Are you threatening me?"

Helton emerged, gun in hand, from Cabin 14. "Shut up—*now!*"

"You certainly haven't handled this at all well," the pilot told the OCO agent.

"You can shut up, too, dear lady." He pointed his stun-gun in Gomez's direction. "Put down all your weapons."

Sighing, Gomez did as instructed. "Up until now, Jake, I really was doing great," he said ruefully.

23

They climbed, slowly, up the twisting hillside path. On their right rose a thick tropical forest, filled with a humid darkness and with the sounds of restless unseen animals and night birds. On the left was a dark, deep and brush-filled ravine. Gomez, still in the uniform he'd borrowed from the skyliner android, was at the head of the single-file procession. Behind him trudged Helton, the blond OCO agent, and then came Jake. The fourth member of the ascending group was Almita.

"I've got both my lazguns back now, *cabrón*," she informed Jake as she stuck the barrel of one of the guns into his back. "Try something smartass now, why don't you?"

"I'm conserving my strength," he said over his shoulder. "For my next assault on you."

"Do it right now, c'mon."

Helton said, "That will be quite enough of that, dear."

"You should have let me change back into my clothes again," complained Gomez, stumbling again. "These trousers are too long."

"Be thankful you're not wearing a shroud."

"At least a shroud wouldn't have legs that are several inches too long." He tripped over one of the dragging pants cuffs.

"Speaking of shrouds," said Jake. "Are you planning to arrange a fatal accident for us?"

"I'd like to do something fatal," put in Almita, poking him with the other gun. "It wouldn't be an accident, either."

"Keep in mind," Helton told her, "that I'm in charge of this soiree." He swung the literod he was carrying in his left hand around, touching her with its wide, intense beam. "As to your inquiry, Cardigan—you're simply going to be detained here for a spell."

"How long a spell?"

He used the literod to illuminate the narrow uphill trail. "No more than a few days."

"That means that whatever's going to be happening in Spain will happen within the next few days."

The OCO man chuckled. "I don't know anything about Spain," he answered.

"You hold us here for a while—then what?"

"You'll be released," he answered. "Provided you haven't succeeded in annoying anyone too much."

"Really? And suppose I report you to—"

"You'll find that I don't exist, Cardigan. None of us do," explained Helton. "Well, except for Almita, and I really doubt you'll be able to track her down."

"The Office of Clandestine Operations will deny you're on the payroll, huh?"

"I'm not on anybody's—"

"*Caramba.*" Gomez had tripped once more, this time sprawling facedown on the trail.

"Get up." Helton turned the light on him. "Very slowly, and without a single try at a trick, get on your feet."

"Trick? *Dios,* I nearly break my favorite leg and you accuse me of—"

"Pay careful attention to me, Gomez," cut in the agent, angry. "I'm very tired of this. Should you slip or stumble once more—I'll stungun you. Then your partner can carry you the rest of the way.

"Behave, Sid," urged Jake. "I'm not up to lugging you."

"I'll try not to fall over, *amigo.* But these baggy pants—"

"We'll continue on our travels," ordered Helton. "We've only got two miles to go."

"That's a long way to trek in pants that don't fit."

After they'd climbed a few minutes in silence, with the beam of Helton's literod illuminating the pathway ahead, Jake inquired, "How'd you get the skyliner to set down here?"

"That's a trade secret."

"The equipment here on the island?"

Helton chuckled. "If it was, it wouldn't be by the time you can get back with anybody official," he said. "Actually, though, it's elsewhere, considerably elsewhere."

"And you got us here without leaving a trace?"

"To the outside world, Cardigan, your disappearance is a mystery. The vanishing skyliner is probably a thirty-second vidnews squib just about now."

"Eventually, I figure—"

"*Ai, caramba!*" Gomez took a new, violent fall. He toppled off the path completely. Crying out once, he went rolling down into the dark foliage-filled ravine on their left.

You could hear him rolling and tumbling down through the darkness.

Helton stepped to the edge of the trail and shined the beam into the gap. There was no sign of Gomez and no sound came up from below.

"That *cabrón*. I'll fix him." Almita, a lazgun in each hand, pivoted and moved to the trail edge.

Jake moved to her side and bumped against her just as she fired. Both shots went up into the humid darkness and not into the ravine where Gomez had vanished.

"Bastard!"

"That'll be enough shooting," ordered Helton. He turned the light on the pathway again.

"Let me go down and find him."

"No, no, dear. We'll deliver Cardigan now."

"What about that asshole running around loose down there?"

"This is a very short-term escape," Helton assured her. "I'll send some people to bring him back later on." He nodded at Jake. "They'll probably have to hurt him. But it can't be helped."

24

Gardner Munsey's skycar didn't warn him at all. It landed on the misty two A.M. landing area atop his apartment building on the fashionable edge of New Baltimore and told him, "Area secure, sir."

"Thank you." He activated the door, ducked out of the skycar and onto the roof.

All the lights died and he was surrounded by darkness.

"Why'd you kill him?"

The door had shut behind him and now the skycar ceased to function.

Munsey narrowed his eyes, squinting into the darkness. He couldn't make out the figure standing over by the ebony skyvan.

"You'll have to be more specific, I'm afraid. Who am I supposed to have shuffled off?"

"Dennis Barragray."

Munsey took a few steps toward the figure. "Is that you, LeeAnn? Why all this—"

"You're supposed to be cooperating with my branch of OCO, Gardner," said LeeAnn Rhymer.

"I am, although my people don't know it." He glanced around the darkened roof. "Very impressive, this. You took care of the secsystems, the lights, my—"

"Why was Barragray killed?"

"I haven't the faintest notion, old girl. It wasn't my work, nor that of any of my people out there in Greater LA."

"You didn't take the money?"

"Which money?"

"The two million dollars in antique paper money he had set aside."

Munsey shook his head. "Did you catch that? I'm shaking my head negatively," he announced into the darkness.

"Barragray was essential to getting all the Devlin Guns shipped to—"

"All the guns have been delivered. So, actually, he was of no further use to—"

"It's not good policy to assassinate people on his level after they've helped us."

"My feelings too, old girl. Which is why I had nothing to do with the poor fellow's demise." He coughed into his hand. "Ought you be here—it's not exactly discreet?"

"Who did kill him?"

"At the moment I can only guess."

"Who?"

"The young woman he was living with off and on at the posh hideaway."

"No, that doesn't make sense. She was working with Zabicas's people to make certain the guns were delivered to—"

"Was she, now?"

"You know that, Gardner."

"What I actually know, old girl, it that she convinced you, and some of those halfwits you work for, that such was the case."

"You don't believe her? Her story checked out completely."

He shrugged. "Did you see that? I shrugged," he said. "She's an actor, and I never trust actors."

"I don't believe she killed him."

"Even if she didn't, she may well have made off with the loot. It's only two million, yet—"

"I'd like it located."

Munsey said, "I'm planning to hop over to Spain tomorrow. I believe she's back in Madrid by now."

"Look her up, Gardner, and retrieve the money."

"For the agency?"

"Deliver it to me, then we'll talk about its final destination."

He smiled thinly. "I'm smiling a skeptical smile, old girl," he told her. "Are you really certain that you trust me?"

"This'll be a way of finding out."

Munsey coughed again. "What about that oaf Sam Trinity? I'm getting awfully weary of having to report to him and take orders from—"

"He won't be with us much longer."

"Yes, so you promised when I initially agreed to participate in this farrago. Sam, however, continues to flourish and is still bossing me. He continues to insist that I rendezvous with him at the offensive whorehouse he—"

"Has Cardigan been taken care of?"

"That he has, old girl, along with his whimsical partner," answered the agent. "They're going to be spending a few delightful days languishing on the island of Fayal in the picturesque Azores, LeeAnn."

"And he wasn't harmed in any way?"

"Not in the least, even though he and Gomez stun-gunned one of our agents."

She told him, "Make certain they both survive. After the coup, they're to be set free."

"Like caged birds, of course. I'll see to it," he promised. "And I'll locate the money for you—or perhaps for *us*. I may even have time to determine who did in poor Barragray. Would you like me to handle that, too?"

There was only silence in reply.

"LeeAnn?"

The lights popped back on, flooding the rooftop with brightness. Munsey was alone.

25

Gomez came to a sudden, rattling stop at what felt like the bottom of the dark ravine. Disentangling himself from a splash of spiky brush, he scrambled to his feet. Taking a deep breath, he tugged off his borrowed trousers, wadded them up and lobbed them off into the thick surrounding darkness. Actually, although he'd informed their captors otherwise, he was wearing his own clothes under the appropriated uniform.

Crouching low, he moved carefully to the left along the now level ground.

He glanced up behind him. Far off on the night trail the bunch that had Jake was moving on and away. The beams of the literods were pointing along the trail and not down into the dark ravine.

There was no sign of pursuit.

"Those *pendejos* must feel confident they can collect me at their leisure," Gomez said to himself as he continued making his way through the tangle of foliage at the gorge bottom. "Still, it was worth making a try at escaping. And possibly the fabled Gomez cunning will help me elude them."

He had a rough idea of the layout of the island and he knew the city of Horta ought to be only a few miles from here.

"If I can make it there, I ought to be able to get word to Bascom and get some troops in here to help me spring Jake from this band of *cabróns*."

Unless the entire population of this small Portuguese island was in cahoots with the Office of Clandestine Operations.

"Nope, that's not likely."

He halted for a moment, listening. Birds were calling off in the sultry darkness. Gomez could hear brush rattling, leaves rustling.

"Apparently I woke up at least half the neighborhood fauna."

He yanked off the uniform coat, wadded that and flung it to the right. Then Gomez continued on his way.

He was navigating by the stars and felt confident, well, fairly confident, that he was heading toward civilization.

"Or at least what passes for civilization in these parts."

He traveled through the tropical night for another five minutes before he became aware of the new sounds behind him.

It was a steady thumping, mixed with the crackling of underbrush. Then, growing louder, came a thin humming noise.

Something was running down through the darkness, following his trail.

"Would that I'd been able to keep at least one weapon." Gomez increased his pace, but didn't break into a run yet.

The methodical thumping was getting closer, louder.

"Robot hunting dogs," he guessed. "At least two of them."

They had picked up his scent, then closed in on his aura. It was a good bet that they'd catch up with him before too long.

Even so, Gomez started to run.

"Cozy," remarked Jake.

"Quite cozy indeed," agreed Agent Helton "And, considering we're underground beneath a banana plantation, it's a much nicer detention cell than you've any right to expect."

The small room was laid out like a parlor, with comfortable black and white furniture, carpeting and drapery. The narrow viewindow showed a sundrenched stretch of the American Southwest.

"Why should this bastard be comfortable?" Almita had

come into the cell with them and was leaning, arms folded under her breasts, against the wall.

Ignoring her, Helton continued, "The sofa and armchair are real. The bookcases are holos, meaning you can't read any of those colorful old novels."

"How long a stay am I registered for?"

"Only a few days, as I mentioned earlier, Cardigan."

"What about my partner?"

Helton's pale blond eyebrows rose slightly. He gave a small shrug, saying, "All depends on the man's attitude. He won't be killed, however, if that's what you're—"

"Don't be too sure," cut in Almita. "If I help track down that son of a bitch, he'll—"

"Enough, dear." Helton took hold of her right arm, just above the elbow. "We've already sent the dogs to find your chum and bring him here."

"Bot dogs?"

"They're gentle souls," assured the OCO agent. "They're set to do no damage. No serious damage."

Nodding, Jake sat on an arm of the low black sofa. "How come you guys are in cahoots with a bastard like Zabicas?"

"Oh, but we aren't, Cardigan. The OCO wouldn't think of collaborating with a notorious foreign Teklord whose—"

"He's a better man than you are, Cardigan." Almita, angry, had pulled free of the restraining hand of the agent. She moved close to Jake, raising a hand to slap him across the face.

As she swung, Jake caught her wrist. He levered her

around, yanked the arm up behind her back and then shoved her in Helton's direction. As she stumbled against the OCO man, Jake suggested, "Maybe you better lock her up for the night."

"*Cabrón!*" She reached for a pocket that held one of her lazguns.

"Don't, please." Helton's stungun was in his hand, the tip of the barrel touching Almita's temple. "Say goodnight to Cardigan, dear."

Spinning on her heel, saying nothing, Almita went striding out of the room and into the grey metal corridor.

"The fridge is also real," said Helton, "should you care for a snack. If you mind your manners, Cardigan, you'll do easy time here and things will be pleasant for us all."

"Including Almita?"

Frowning, Helton said, "You know how unpleasant necessity can be at times."

"Why's it necessary to help Teklords smuggle guns?"

Helton smiled. "Your viewindow is equipped with fifty six appealing vistas," he said, backing to the doorway. "In case you want something to do. Goodnight."

GOMEZ FELL DOWN again.

This time he'd caught his foot in a thick twist of root. He tripped, feeling a sudden jab of pain in his ankle, and then went falling over into the darkness.

He hit on his side, new pains shooting through his ribs. His teeth rattled and the breath went sighing out of him.

Gasping, he dug in with his right elbow and got himself to a sitting position. He turned just in time to see one of the pursuing robot dogs launch itself at him.

It was the size of a police dog, made of silvery metal that gave off a faint glow. Its wide jaw was filled with sharp metal teeth, many more than a normal dog came equipped with. Its plaz eyes glowed an intense red and sent two thin crimson beams of light right at his chest. The dog seemed to be drifting through the night, aimed straight at him.

Gomez swallowed hard as he flattened out on his back.

The heavy robot dog hound went sailing clean over him to land a few feet away.

Gomez struggled upward, feeling new pains as he put weight on his injured ankle. He spun to face the glowing metal dog.

Its slow metallic humming sounded increasingly like an angry growl.

The winded detective managed to grab a heavy stone from the ground. "Scram, *perro*," he suggested, "or I'll bop you with this."

The creature eyed him, legs spread wide and silvery head tucked low.

Suddenly something hit Gomez terribly hard in the middle of his back.

He went staggering forward, arms flapping wide, dropping the rock.

The second of the pursuing robot dogs had jumped at him. Its metal forepaws smacked him between the shoulder blades.

Crouched, he turned to face the second hound. He held out both hands toward the thing. "Back, *perro*."

The dog lunged, leaped, caught hold of his right wrist. The sharp metal teeth dug into Gomez's skin.

The bot made a noise that sounded like "Yawp." Its jaws snapped open. It let go of Gomez's bloody wrist and dropped to the ground. The lights died behind its eyes and it lay still.

"Still one more metallic mutt to go." Perplexed, Gomez made it to his feet again.

The other dog was lying stiff and still on its silvery metallic side just to the left of Gomez.

26

What were you expecting to accomplish, *Senhor* Gomez?"

"From the way you pronounce *señor*, I'd judge you to be Portuguese."

"*Sim.*"

"Wellsir, I saw a chance to get away from some goons and I took it," said Gomez. "Which side are you on in this fracas, by the way?"

The lean young man was about thirty, wearing dark trousers and a black pullover. "I'm sure you've heard of Pax International." He was standing a few feet away, an odd-looking gun dangling in his left hand.

"Privately funded bunch of do-gooders."

He laughed. "You ought to be grateful I was around to do you good, Gomez."

"I was saving the gratitude until I was dead sure you're not simply an OCO yunkus posing as a do-gooder," said the detective. "Or maybe a Teklord heavy. How come you know my name?"

"I have a good memory."

"We've met?"

"No, but I study a lot of dossiers. That was Jake Cardigan up there with you, wasn't it?"

"*Sí.* And who are you?"

"Jose Silveira."

"A local lad?"

"No, I'm from the continent. Lisbon."

"And just hanging around the jungle waiting for a chance to be helpful?"

"Tell me why you're here, Gomez," countered Silveira.

"We had not much choice." Gomez, while he wrapped his bloody wrist in a plyochief, explained the events leading up to his being hounded through the night jungle on this particular island in the Atlantic. "And you?"

"I'm with the branch of Pax that's devoted to discouraging the spread of illicit arms," he answered. "There's a temporary way station here on Fayal. I've been keeping an eye on it for the past few weeks."

"Do you hole up hereabouts?"

"*Sí,* I have a hideaway nearby."

"Might I suggest, *amigo,* that we adjourn there now?" He looked beyond the other man and at the surrounding dark jungle.

"That's probably a good notion, Gomez. They'll be getting curious as to why their dogs haven't reported in lately." He gestured with the gun in his left hand. "We have to cut through the brush over that way."

"What'd you use to discourage those hounds?"

"It's a new type of sonblaster." Silveira started moving into the brush. "Once in a while I keep a sample from a batch of weapons we've confiscated."

"Handy." Nodding, Gomez followed him.

JAKE WAS FINISHING up his second circuit of the cozy cell. He'd located two hidden monitor cams so far, one up in the simulated stucco ceiling and one behind the holographic floor-to-ceiling bookcases. There was also a backup audio bug under the holo endtable.

Tongue poked in cheek, he sat on the sofa and gazed upward. Getting out of here was going to be tricky.

The door of the cell suddenly whispered open.

Almita, dropping an electrokey into her trouser pocket, slipped into the parlor.

The door shut behind her.

"I thought you were forbidden to drop in," he said.

"They don't know I'm here, asshole."

"Sure they do." He pointed a thumb at the concealed overhead cam.

She smiled, coming closer. She jabbed her right hand into her jacket pocket. "I jammed the secsystem for this whole section."

"Won't take them long to find that out."

"I only need a couple minutes to take care of you." Her hand came out clutching one of her lazguns. "There's no reason to keep you alive, Cardigan."

"I can think of several."

"So can these OCO *mariposas*." The gunhand came up. "You don't want to make the OCO unhappy. They—"

All at once Jake was no longer on the sofa. He had dived to the left of Almita, hitting the floor about five feet from her.

"Cabrón!"

As she swung around to get a shot at him, he dived.

He tackled her waist high, at the same time smacking her wrist with the side of his hand.

She cried out, fingers splaying, dropping the gun.

It hit the holographic endtable and fell right through it to the floor.

Almita struggled to get her second gun out.

The two of them fell back toward the bookcases. Almita hit first and seemed to blend into the rows of bright-covered books.

Jake broke free of her, then caught hold of the front of her jacket.

He pulled her toward him with his left hand and dealt three hard jabs to her approaching chin.

Her teeth made a grinding sound. She groaned, lost consciousness. Almita fell back against the holographic bookcase again, slid down through the images of books.

Jake knelt on one knee, grabbing the lazgun from her pocket and thrusting it in his belt. Then he took the electrokey she'd used to get into his cell.

After collecting the second lazgun and slipping that in his belt beside the other one, Jake sprinted to the door.

There wasn't going to be much time left before they got the secsystem working again.

He used the key. The door whirred and slid open.

Standing in the grey corridor with his lazgun aimed directly at Jake was Agent Helton. "I was coming to rescue you from Almita, Cardigan," he said, smiling. "Apparently that won't be necessary."

27

The second robot guard came tumbling down. His gunmetal body slammed into the ground with a rattling thud.

"It also works pretty well on humanoid robots," mentioned Silveira, holstering the sonblaster.

"So I noticed." Gomez was standing beside the first of the fallen bot guards. "These lads look as dormant as the hounds that were on my tail."

A warm wind was drifting through the jungle. Up in the dark tree branches overhead some unseen birds began to cry mournfully.

"We've got about ten minutes or less to get in and out." He nodded at the immense plastiglass dome that rose up a dozen yards away, covering the sprawling plantation.

From his side pocket Gomez slid the palmtop monitor the Pax agent had loaned him. "According to this spyscreen of yours, Jose, there's still somebody in detention cell 6 on Level C," he said after scanning the small rectangular screen. "I'm betting it's Jake."

Silveira had two small darkmetal discs in his hand. "Wear this, *amigo.*" He fixed a disc to the front of Gomez's jacket, the other to his. "A little gadget that'll confuse the secmonitors down in the tunnels."

"What'll they think they're viewing as we wend our way to Jake?"

"Robot guards."

"Something else you confiscated?"

"No, this one we came up with ourselves." He took hold of Gomez's arm. "The entry to the underground passways is over here. We'll pass under the domewall and come out two levels under the plantation buildings." He moved quietly through the brush. "It'll take us at least five minutes to get to where they seem to be keeping your partner."

"Which means we'll have less than five more to spring Jake and get the heck out of there."

"*Sim.*" Halting and letting go of Gomez, Silveira crouched beside a large flowering bush. "While we're in the corridors, don't say anything. Even with these gadgets, the monitors will detect an unfamiliar voice."

"*Caramba,* I don't know if I can go that long without uttering a single pithy remark."

"Try." He touched a large metal panel embedded in the damp ground.

The panel slid silently aside, revealing a dimlit metal stairway quirking down into the corridors below.

GOMEZ, VERY CAREFULLY, coughed into his hand.

Walking single file, he and Silveira stepped through the doorway to the section of Level C where the detention cells were located.

They'd been in the underground passway exactly six minutes now. Thus far they hadn't encountered anyone, robot or human.

The Pax agent was walking, rapidly, two paces ahead of the detective. He slowed, inclining his head very slightly to the left.

The number etched on the coppery metal door was 2.

Gomez wrinkled his nose. The aircirc system down here on Level C didn't seem to be working exactly right. There was a very strong odor of ripe bananas everywhere.

Or maybe, reflected Gomez, that was what they intended. This was, after all, supposed to be a banana plantation and nothing else.

They passed a door numbered 4.

Silveira halted at the next door. This one was designated 6.

He took out a master electrokey.

Gomez, casually, eased his right hand into the jacket pocket that held his borrowed stungun.

The door slid open.

There was a bright cozy parlor across the threshold, furnished in black and white. There was a comfortable sofa, an armchair and wallhigh bookcases.

But there was no sign of Jake, or anyone else, in the cell.

28

Bascom was looking rumpled again. He was sitting on the edge of his desk, legs dangling, and noodling out a chorus of a twentieth-century bop tune, "Un Poco Loco," on his saxophone.

The desk vidphone buzzed.

The Chief of the Cosmos Detective Agency set the sax aside. "What?" he asked, turning toward the phone-screen.

The image of the metal head of the switchboard bot was wiped off, replaced by Rex/GK-30. "Excuse my barging in on you, Bascom," the robot said. "But these two tykes are getting anxious for news."

Behind the large bot Bascom saw Dan and Molly

standing. "Nothing new since last time we talked, kids," he said, shaking his head sadly.

"Are they alive?" asked Dan.

"There's no report of a crash, Dan," replied Bascom. "I've been urging a few of my contacts back in DC to find out what the OCO knows about this."

"You're sure it is the OCO?"

"At least a contingent of that esteemed organization, yes."

"Aren't you doing anything else?"

"Dan, I've got five of my best operatives on this. And I've put out the word to our informant network. Sooner or—"

"But right now, you aren't even sure if my dad and Sid are still alive?"

"I'm betting that—"

"The Teklords are also involved in this frumus, kiddo," cut in Rex. "Here, take a gander at this gink."

A vidclip of a dark, thickset man filled the screen. The man was walking, head down, across the lobby of a hotel.

"This is Roberto Martinez," explained the robot. "I glommed this from a secsyst cam in the lobby of Hotel Borderland."

"And?"

"Martinez is the bozo who came in, interrupted Molly's ne'er-do-well uncle while he was chinning with her and waltzed the guy out and possibly into oblivion."

"He's connected with one of the Mexican Tek cartels?"

"Yep, the Navarro Cartel, biggest one in Borderland."

Frowning, Bascom tapped the bell of his saxophone. "Usually they hire outside help for these simple chores," he said thoughtfully. "They must've been in a rush to stop—"

"Important holocall coming in," blurted out one of the holograph stages.

"I'll get back to you, Dan. Don't worry."

Bascom crossed to the platform and activated it.

The life-size projection of a man in a yellow suit materialized. He was pudgy and he had no head. There was just a blurred ball of pale blue light resting on his shoulders. "I understand you're interested in the present whereabouts of Jake Cardigan and Sid Gomez, Bascom. True?"

Making a slow half circuit of the stage, Bascom said, "You don't usually deal in this sort of information, Wordsworth."

"I came across this gem of intelligence by chance," said the headless informant. "Being dedicated to the cause of justice, I decided to risk my anonymity by contacting you in person in this manner."

"How much?"

"Naturally my first concern is the safety of your operatives and—"

"Your price?"

A coughing noise came out of the blur. "Five thousand dollars."

"Three thousand tops."

"I know where your ops are languishing, Bascom.
"Forty-five hundred."

"Thirty-five hundred."

"Four thousand dollars or I depart."

"Deal. Now tell me where—"

"Jesus! Got to go. Stand by until later, Bascom." There
was a faint popping sound and Wordsworth was gone.

"Shit," observed Bascom.

AGENT HELTON'S OFFICE was small, crowded with too many
metal chairs, databoxes, neowood packing crates and
bundles of old faxmemos. His desk was wedged in a corner and there were two dozen small vidscreens in the
walls to the left and right of it. "You're not paying attention, Cardigan," he complained from the metal chair that
was jammed behind the narrow gunmetal desk.

"I'm still admiring the decor." Jake was straddling a
chair, facing the OCO man.

"This is a temp setup, purely functional." He gestured
at a bank of viewscreens to his left. "What do you see
there?"

"Assorted views of what I assume is the jungle outside,
shot with nitecams."

Nodding slowly, Helton said, "What you don't see,
however, is as much as a trace of your damned missing
partner."

"True," agreed Jake.

"Notice Screen Seventeen."

This showed a white metal lab table, brightlit from overhead, upon which sprawled a large robot dog.

"Defunct dog," said Jake.

"That's one of the two highly efficient robot tracking dogs that were sent to locate Gomez, incapacitate him and then signal our people," continued Helton. "They never fail."

"Until tonight."

"Both of these dogs were rendered inoperative by a highly sophisticated sonic weapon." He put both elbows on the desk, leaning forward, eyeing Jake. "Where'd Gomez get such a weapon?"

"The gift shop at the skyport?"

Helton's frown deepened. "Do you bastards have allies on this island?"

"Sure. We sent a whole troop of them here on the off chance we'd someday be highjacked." He grinned. "C'mon, Helton, be rational. I have no idea what Gomez used on your mechanized mutts."

"I want him here." He tapped the desktop with a blunt forefinger. "He has to be brought in—now."

"So keep looking for him."

The agent said, "No, you're going to help me round him up, Cardigan."

"No, I'm not, nope."

"My instructions are not to harm you, not seriously," he told Jake. "Still, we have some gadgets here that—"

"How about a Devlin Gun?" asked Jake. "That might scare me into cooperating."

After exhaling slowly, then inhaling, Helton advised him, "You don't want to know anything about the Devlin Guns."

Jake said, "Almita's working for Carlos Zabicas. He's got the guns and—"

"Zabicas hasn't got them."

"Oh, so? Then who did you guys arrange to—"

"Right now all you have to worry about is helping me get Gomez herded in here." Helton stood. "We're going out into the jungle, you and I, Cardigan, and—"

"And I'm what—bait?"

"Yeah, exactly."

Jake shook his head. "I decline."

"Then I'll have to persuade you."

Jake asked, "How high up in the OCO does this go? Who told you to waylay us but not knock us off?"

Smiling, Helton answered, "Maybe nobody ordered me to spare your lives," he suggested. "Perhaps I'm simply conning you, Cardigan. It might be that your only real chance of surviving depends on your helping me locate Gomez. Otherwise—"

"No need to come hunting for me, *cabrón*." Gomez came striding into the office, stungun in hand. "You okay, Jake?"

"Fit as a fiddle."

"Then we'll— No, *hombre*." Gomez had noticed Helton reaching toward a shoulder holster. He fired the stungun.

Helton took a jerking step back, bumped into the wall. Both his elbows went snapping back, one nudging into a viewscreen and shattering it. He gave a brief gargling cry, then pitched over onto his desk, scattering faxmemos and datadiscs.

"This would be a dandy time to depart, *amigo.*" Gomez headed for the door. "If you've no objections."

"None." Jake followed his partner.

29

Silveira pointed up the dark hillside. "There's a little town called Castel' Branco about another three miles from here," he told them. "If we can get there, I'll be able to set you up with a skyvan."

"*If?*" inquired Gomez as they started double-timing up a twisting roadway that was cut through rocky ground. "Can't you be a bit more optimistic, *amigo?*"

"Well, they must know by now that Jake's gone. They'll be sending out as many people as they can spare to track us."

Jake said, "This isn't going to help your standing on the island much."

"Nobody spotted me while Gomez got you out of there. It'll be safe for me to stay around awhile longer."

They climbed in silence for several minutes.

Then from the darkness far below near the plantation came a faint chuffing sound.

"Skycars," said Jake.

"At least two of them," added Gomez.

Silveira halted. From a trouser pocket he took three small black squares of plaz. "Fix one of these to your clothes," he told them, passing a square to each and slapping one to his jacket. "It'll block your aura and fool their sensors."

"If they use litebeams, they may spot us anyhow," said Jake.

"We'll have to make sure they don't." Silveira sprinted across the roadway and into the tangle of jungle that stretched away beside it.

When they were in among the trees and flowering brush, Gomez said, "Maybe we should've tried to take back the skyliner."

"Too many guards." Silveira led them up through the night woodlands.

The sound of the skycar engines was growing louder. Looking back, Jake saw three of them drifting up through the darkness. The headlights bobbing like lanterns in the wind. From the belly of each craft came a wide beam of intense bluish light. The skycars were moving slowly at a height of about 200 feet, sweeping the ground below them with light.

The cars separated after a moment. Two of them headed inland and the third kept heading up toward Jake and his companions.

"That one'll be overhead in about a minute," said the Pax agent. "We better flatten out under the brush."

Gomez stretched out in a tangle of spiky bushes. "Oops," he muttered. "I think I'm reclining amidst the remains of some animal friend's snack."

Jake was ducked down a few feet from his partner.

In less than thirty seconds the skycar was directly above the three men.

The beam of glaring light slowly and methodically probed at the jungle all around them. The car seemed to hover there for a long time.

But then it moved on, flying uphill and away. Going very slowly, illuminating the jungle as it went.

Five minutes after it had flown out of sight, Silveira said quietly, "*Muito bem*. We can try for Castel' Branco now." He rose up out of the tangle of brush he'd been hiding in.

Gomez stood, brushing at the front of his jacket with a handful of leaves. "I wonder if we can find a haberdasher open at this hour," he said.

SHOWING NO LIGHTS. Gomez guided the skyvan up into the darkness above the sleeping town.

The black craft rose quietly up and away from the island.

In the passenger seat Jake was hunched slightly and studying a scanner screen on the dash panel. "According to this, all three of those skycars are over on the other side of the island."

"Let us attempt to sneak away without their tumbling to our departure."

Gomez kept the skyvan at a low altitude until they were out over the dark Atlantic. Then he gradually climbed up to 10,000 feet.

Jake said, "Looks like we're away clear."

Gomez turned on the flying lights. "Remind me to send Jose a faxcard next Xmas," he said. "He was very helpful to the cause of Gomez preservation."

"Find out anything new about the shipment of Devlin Guns?"

"He's of the opinion that several crates of them were routed through here."

"Bound for Spain?"

"Far as he knows, which confirms what we've already been pretty sure of."

"During my chat with Helton I played dumb and—"

"That must've required a heck of a lot of acting ability on your part, *amigo*."

Jake grinned. "Good thing I'm aware that these jabs at my character are due to the stress you've been through recently," he said. "The point is, I suggested that Zabicas Cartel was the destination for the Devlin Guns."

"Did he confirm or deny?"

"He let slip that the guns went to somebody other than Zabicas."

"Meaning that Natalie Dent's tip is probably right," said Gomez. "The weapons went to Janeiro Martinez and his rebel outfit."

"Probably, yeah. But since Almita works for Zabicas

and has considerable interest in putting us out of business, we still have to figure that Zabicas is involved in whatever's coming up in Madrid and environs."

"If our recent hosts weren't spoofing us, these events are due any day now," speculated Gomez. "They implied they only wanted us sidelined for a week at most."

Jake tapped the vidphone. "I'll contact Bascom," he said. "Tell him we're back on the job and also where Quixote Airlines can pick up their missing skyliner." He punched out the number of the Cosmos Detective Agency in Greater LA. "Then I'll let Dan know we're okay."

"Our esteemed *jefe* may also want to alert certain DC cronies about this little island paradise OCO outpost."

Jake shrugged. "Helton and his crew are probably packing already," he said. "By the time those dimwits in Washington take action, there won't be anything at the banana plantation but bananas."

Bascom's face appeared on the phonescreen. "Jake," he said, giving a pleased smile. "I'm glad to see you. You've saved me from having to pay an informant four thousand bucks."

30

It was raining in Madrid. A heavy slanting rain that was hitting hard at the blue skycar.

"Considering all the expense Newz, Inc., went to in overhauling you, not that they aren't wading in money, since they never pay their crackerjack reporters anything near what—"

"Wallowing."

"Hum?"

"Wallowing in money, not wading."

Natalie Dent shifted slightly in the passenger seat, running her thumb knuckle along her freckled nose. "Now see? There you go again, Sidebar, exhibiting the caustic wit that I associate with a streetwise reprobate of the order of Sid Gomez and—"

"A putz."

"I'd hoped, as I've been trying to convey, despite your constant snide interruptions, that being rebuilt and reconstructed would have modified your character some. It strikes me, and I am, afterall, perceptive enough to be considered one of the best, if not *the* best, investigative reporters in the vidnews business, that a robot such as yourself, Sidebar, ought to know his place and not be continually—"

"My place is to be an ace cameraman." Sidebar was piloting the Newz, Inc., skycar through the rainswept Madrid afternoon. "Not to chauffeur you around this rinkydink town."

"Madrid isn't, by any stretch of the imagination, rinkydink." Natalie shook her head, causing her long red hair to brush her shoulders. "We are, afterall, comrades in arms, as it were, and you ought to be glad to do me a good turn now and then, especially since our regular pilot is laid up with some sort of rare virus."

"Booze isn't a rare virus." The robot punched out a landing pattern. "We're over the Calle Mayor. And there's the side street where that abysmal monstrosity the Hotel Condor aspires above the—"

"I think it's rather cute."

"That it is."

The car glided down through the rain and landed on Parking Lot Quatro, which was next to the towering silver metal and black plastiglass Hotel Condor.

"I trust, Sidebar, that you won't simply sit here and sulk while I'm in the Cafe Picasso talking to Secretary of

State Torres. Use the time to improve your mind or to meditate, which, I understand, is as valuable for mechanical brains as it is for—"

"My calling in life is to take insightful pictures." The robot tapped the vidcamera built into his chest. "Not sit on my toke and listen to the raindrops falling on—"

"Secretary Torres wants to talk to me privately. That's what he said when he called this morning."

"Privately in a hotel restaurant?"

"We're operating, as I shouldn't have to point out, in the realm of the political intrigue here," said the red-haired reporter. "Señor Torres wants this to look like a perfectly routine interview, yet he doesn't want any of it going on the record. I should think by now, having ably assisted me on a variety of highly complex and dangerous investigative reporting missions, Sidebar, you'd be in possession of a heck of a lot more political savvy." Sighing, she unfastened the safety gear, tugged a small force-field umbrella from her coat pocket and stepped out into the rainy afternoon.

"I'M SUFFERING FROM a bad case of granulated eyeballs," mentioned Gomez as he headed the skyvan down toward Parking Lot Quatro.

"Thought it was your ankle and your wrist that got bunged up on the island."

"I'm suffering from those battle scars, too, now that you mention it. But lack of rest and sleep is also taking its toll."

"I had the impression you were snoozing away while the van was on automatic en route here to Spain."

"I slept fitfully," explained Gomez as their vehicle settled down onto a landing space. "I've never stayed at the Hotel Condor before, but Bascom assures me it's a deluxe establishment."

"Have to be to get away with that façade."

Gomez asked, "You still going to concentrate on locating the multifaceted Janine?"

"Initially, yeah. While you start tracing the Devlin Guns."

"First thing for me to do is make certain they ended up with Janeiro Martinez—and then find out where he's got them stashed." Unhooking his safety gear, Gomez nudged the door open. He was halfway out into the rain, when he sat back down again, sideways, legs hanging out in the downpour. "Do my bleary eyes deceive me, *amigo*, or is that indeed a Newz, Inc., crate over yonder?"

Jake glanced in the direction his partner was pointing. "Looks to be."

Gomez nodded forlornly. "I didn't think I'd be encountering my nemesis so soon," he said. "But I recognize the smug camerabot sitting there in the car. It's Sidebar, known accomplice of Natalie Dent. That means, alas, that the lady herself must be in the vicinity."

"You'll get soggy perched there, Sid. Let's get inside the damn hotel."

"Fate is a peculiar thing," observed Gomez as he

stepped completely out of the skyvan. "It never throws me into the path of sweet-tempered and highly intelligent young women, but rather strews my uphill path with—"

"A highly intelligent young woman would head for shelter the moment you came within range."

"Another nasty trick that fate plays on me," said Gomez, "is to pair me with a partner who doesn't appreciate my immense charm."

A few spaces to their right the pilotside window of the Newz, Inc., skycar opened a quarter. "Hi there, putz," called the robot cameraman.

"Welcome to Madrid," muttered Gomez, heading for the hotel entrance.

THE CAFE PICASSO was a large multilevel place adjacent to the vast soaring lobby of the Hotel Condor. Natalie and the short pudgy secretary of state had taken a table on the level that featured a replica of Pablo Picasso's studio built on a floating platform. An androidsim of an aged Picasso was at work at an easel, clad only in a pair of khaki shorts and sandals.

Turning away from watching the android, Secretary Torres said, "A very fascinating artist. Full of fire."

"He's okay," said Natalie.

"Before we leave, we'll go up to the top level of the cafe and see the animated *Guernica*." From his breast pocket he took a bright orange plyochief and dabbed at his perspiring forehead. "I find myself, my dear, in an un-

pleasant position. Not merely unpleasant but dangerous."

She rested one arm on the small table, which had a Picasso dove etched on its plastiglass surface. Leaning
closer to the politician, Natalie said, "This has to do with
what we talked about the other day, Señor Torres?"

He wiped his forehead. "*Sí*, my dear," he replied. "The
guns, *sí*. On that previous occasion I made light of your
suggestions that the Garcia regime was going to be the
target of an imminent coup."

"You were perspiring a lot then, too, Mr. Secretary,"
reminded Natalie, watching the pudgy man. "Being a
seasoned reporter, I knew you weren't being absolutely
honest and forthright with me."

"*Es verdad*," admitted Torres. "I already knew that
weapons of some kind had been delivered to Janeiro
Martinez, that he was planning to use them in an attempt
to overthrow our government."

"Does President Garcia know what you know? I assume, as a trusted member of his cabinet, you'd have—"

"The situation, *señorita*, is a complex one, very deli-
cate," he said, wiping at his forehead with the orange plyochief. "One has a loyalty to one's country, but also to
oneself."

"So you haven't discussed this with Garcia?"

"There are several factors to consider," said Torres,
glancing again at the android Picasso. "For one thing,
your American government is involved."

"I know about the Office of Clandestine Operations."

"It goes somewhat higher than that. There is, I am

fairly certain, someone high in the Interim Cabinet, which was established after your president was forced to resign. Someone in that cabinet who is active in what's going on."

Natalie sat up. "I didn't know that. Who?"

"I am unable to say. However, I know that a certain segment of the United States government wants President Garcia out of power." He wiped at his forehead with the orange plyochief. "I'll go, too. But I've been hoping to arrange a safe and comfortable retirement for myself."

"And that's not possible anymore?"

He shook his head slowly and sadly. "I've learned that I won't be allowed to live should the coup succeed," he said. "That is a very sobering reality to have to adjust to."

"I won't allow anything like that to happen," she said, angry. "I'll use the power of vidnews to expose—"

"There is a quicker and, from my point of view, more helpful way to approach this, *señorita*," the perspiring secretary of state cut in. "If your esteemed Newz, Inc., organization could arrange me safe passage to elsewhere—and provide me with sufficient funds—I'd be willing to provide them information."

"What exactly do you have to sell?"

Glancing for a few seconds at the painting android, he turned back to her. "A brilliant artist, so confident and sure of himself," he observed. "But then, the twentieth century was a more confident age than ours."

"What is it you're selling, Mr. Secretary?"

"I know the reasons your government wants us out of power."

"That's easy to guess. The OCO, or at least part of it, wants to encourage the Tek trade again in these parts. Garcia's administration has been cracking down on—"

"Ah, but it's much more complicated than that, my dear." Torres lowered his voice. "Zabicas has promised to . . ." He half rose in his chair, staring toward the artist's studio. "*Deus!*"

Picasso had tossed his brush aside. From the waistband of his shorts he drew a lazgun. Spinning, smiling, he aimed the gun at the table where Torres and Natalie were sitting.

31

Gomez had spotted her first. "*Ai*, it's just as I feared," he remarked, slowing as they crossed the many-tiered lobby.

"What?" inquired Jake.

"The bane of my life, sitting in the restaurant yonder with— *Caramba!*"

Leaving Jake, Gomez went running across the lobby and up the ramp to the second level of the Cafe Picasso. He'd noticed the artist android discard his brush and reach for the lazgun tucked into his waistband.

The racing detective reached Natalie Dent's table just as Picasso aimed and fired.

Gomez tackled the redhaired reporter and they both fell to the right and hit the floor in a tangle.

Secretary Torres cried out a thin keening scream when the beam of the lazgun sliced into his chest.

Rolling free of the sprawled Natalie, Gomez snapped out his stungun and fired at the android.

The beam hit the mechanical Picasso while he was swinging around to take aim at the fallen reporter.

The andy's arms snapped to his sides, the lazgun fell to the simulated studio floor, bounced twice. Picasso tottered forward, teetered on the edge of the platform for several seconds before plunging over onto a table just below.

"You in passable shape, *chiquita?*" Gomez inquired, holstering his gun, and offered her a hand.

"Yes, fine, thanks, Gomez. I'll express my gratitude later." She waved away his assistance, pulling a palmphone out of her skirt pocket. Punching out a number, she said, "Sidebar, get the heck in here on the triple. There's just been an assassination and we're the first ones on the scene."

COLONEL MARESCA OF the Policia National was a tall, lean man of fifty. His crisp tan uniform was trimmed in gold and there were many bright medals and ribbons on the chest of the jacket. His large circular office was at the top of the Justicia building on the Plaza De La Independencia. From his high, wide viewindow you could see a portion of the simulated greenery of Retiro Park below.

Jake said, "Not a damn thing."

Turning away from the window, the colonel returned to his realwood desk and stood beside it. "I have, Señor Cardigan, heard many favorable things about you," he said, smiling briefly. "It is said that, despite your earlier criminal career, you have an excellent reputation as a private investigator who—"

"What I don't have, Colonel, is an earlier criminal career." Jake was slouched in an armchair near the wide desk. "That was a Teklord frame. You can find all the details in—"

"Of course, *sí*, forgive me." Maresca smiled apologetically. "I was allowing the fact that you'd served considerable time in an American cryoprison known in the underworld as the Freezer affect my judgment and my memory." He smiled again, even more briefly. "The point I was making is that I find it odd that you, a respected investigator, would withhold information from—"

"I'm not withholding any information, Colonel," Jake assured him. "My partner and I don't know, as I've already said, a damn thing about the assassination of Secretary Torres."

"A true shame that Señor Gomez couldn't make our meeting."

"Since your invitation said this wasn't an official request but just a courtesy thing, he decided to go out and work on the case we're here in Spain to cover."

"And you believe this case, whatever it is, has nothing to do with the murder of the secretary of state?" The colonel sat down behind the desk.

"I'd bet that it does," answered Jake. "But right now, Colonel, I don't know exactly how it ties in. What did Natalie Dent say?"

"You're acquainted with the young lady, I believe?"

"Yep," admitted Jake, "know her well."

"During my recent interview with her, she was her usual circumlocutious self."

Jake grinned. "You think Janeiro Martinez is behind the killing?"

"That's a possibility."

"Where is the guy?"

"That I don't know. He and his core people move about."

"Don't the National Police keep track of their prominent rebels?"

"We try to, Señor Cardigan," said Maresca. "But the fact that Martinez is still not in prison attests that he's very good at outfoxing us."

"What about Carlos Zabicas?"

"A suspected Teklord," said the colonel. "He has a villa, a most impressive one, on the outskirts of the city."

"He's linked with Martinez, isn't he?"

"That's my belief, but there isn't any proof."

"President Garcia's been cracking down on the Tek trade in Spain," said Jake. "That gives Zabicas a motive for wanting him out of office."

"A motive shared by a great many other Teklords."

"Have you questioned Zabicas about his association with Martinez?"

"Zabicas is not an easy man to question."

"You can't invite the guy in for an informal chat like ours, huh?"

Colonel Maresca smiled. "Unfortunately, no, *señor.* You're aware that a great deal of money, no matter how it's made, has the power to insulate one from a great many of the annoyances of society. Including police questions."

Jake nodded. "What about a supply of illegal weapons that recently came into your country?"

"The smuggling of unauthorized weapons is a thriving trade. Can you be more specific?"

"Devlin Guns."

The colonel got up, returning to the window. "We believe that Martinez has them."

"You don't know where?"

"Not at this time, no."

"What would be your guess?"

"I don't make guesses. That's an occupation for private detectives."

Jake stood, too. "Something's going to happen within the next few days, Colonel," he said toward the policeman's back. "The assassination this afternoon must tie in."

"We're already investigating the possibility of an attempt to overthrow President Garcia," Maresca assured him. "*Gracias* for coming in. I'm sorry you weren't able to provide me with more information."

"I was about to say the same thing to you." Giving him a lazy salute, Jake made his way out of the office.

32

Don't go moping along with that hangfrog expression on your aging face. Afterall, I've already expressed—"

"Hangdog. It's a hangdog expression people display when shrouded in gloom, *chiquita*. Not applicable here, since outrage is what I am attempting to—"

"My point, Gomez, and you really seem intent on muddying the waters with a lot of unnecessary verbiage, instead of following the example I always strive to practice and that is to get right to the point without a lot of shilly-shallying around the bush, my point is that I'm obviously grateful to you," said Natalie Dent as they walked side by side along a lane lined with holographic projections of trees. The rain had stopped and the sky over Retiro Park was a yellowish grey. "Afterall, by knocking me to the floor, spilling my soup of the day all over my best skirt in the process, you undoubtedly saved my life and kept that assassin andy from carrying out his full mission." She gave him a cordial pat on the elbow.

"I accept your deftly phrased expression of undying gratitude." The detective glanced back over his shoulder and scowled. "Does your snide cambot have to stick so close to us?"

"Sidebar is also acting, considering all I've been through today, as my official bodyguard. Newz, Inc., orders, which indicates they think a lot more of me than I've been assuming."

The robot, who was walking about ten feet behind them, cupped his metal hands to his voxbox. "I've got exceptional hearing, putz," he called. "A couple more wisearse remarks out of you and—"

"Hush, Sidebar," ordered Natalie, frowning at the bot. "Don't let his sometimes surly attitude annoy you, Gomez. His ill manners are caused by a mechanical quirk that frequent overhauls have failed to detect."

Gomez lowered his voice, saying, "Okay, tell me why somebody wanted both you and Secretary Torres dead?"

"I've been doing a heck of a lot of brooding over that very exact question," the redhaired reporter told him. "It's my impression, and my instincts in situations like this have proven fairly accurate on previous occasions, keep in mind, that the secretary, poor man, was getting ready to tell me something important."

"Do your infallible instincts hint to you as to what it might be?"

"You know that the Office of Clandestine Operations is up to its chin in this gunrunning, don't you?"

"Up to its ears. *Sí.*"

"Secretary Torres was getting ready to reveal, I'm nearly certain, some further motivation for the OCO's involvement in Spanish politics and the operations of the country's largest Tek cartel."

"Money," said Gomez, guiding Natalie over to a wrought-iron bench. "Let's rest while we chat."

"We can't sit on that." She pointed with the toe of her shoe at a low sign.

"Warning!" the sign said in several languages. *"This is but a holo image. Do not attempt to sit."*

"As I was saying, the OCO must be involved in raising money for some other shady operation." He and Natalie continued walking.

"Guerrilla activities are warming up in Brazil again," said the young woman thoughtfully. "And so far, Congress and the Interim President are opposed to supplying any funds."

"Africa's a better bet. Several choice sneaky conflicts underway in—"

Something buzzed in her skirt pocket. "Excuse me a minute, Gomez." She pulled out her palmphone. "Go ahead."

"Hi, Nat. This is Eddie Wexler with *NewsTalk* mag. Got some time for—"

"Hold on for just a second, Eddie." She nudged the

detective in the ribs with her forefinger. "Could you stand over there out of earshot for a bit? This is, I'm sure, going to be an offer from this trashy zine to do a piece on the Torres business. I'd rather you didn't hear me negotiating for money with this goniff, since it might tarnish the bright image you have of me as a sweet and demure person."

"*Sí*, I don't want to shatter anymore illusions than I can help," he said, taking a step away from her. "But, *bonita*, we have yet to talk about the possible whereabouts of Martinez and company."

"We will," she promised. "Now, shoo."

Thrusting his hands in his trouser pockets, Gomez trotted across the lane and stood under a real oak tree.

"Care to play a game of chance while cooling your heels?" called Sidebar.

Gomez replied with an unfriendly sound.

THE OFFICES OF Maravilla Detective Services were in a brand-new building on the Calle Goya. The ninth-floor corridor smelled fresh, and there were two copperplated robots laying carpet down at the far end.

"Señor Cardigan," said the voxbox built into the licorice-colored Lucite desk in the agency reception room as Jake crossed the threshold and the door slid shut behind him. "Señor Soberano will be with you in approximately thirty seconds."

A door in the far wall opened and a short plump man

of about forty smiled out at him. "Come on in, Jake," he invited. "I'm glad you persuaded Bascom to hire us to back you up on this."

Shaking hands, Jake said, "We have a rich client, so I figured we could afford the inflated fees you guys charge, Pavo."

"Maravilla is known throughout Europe for its reasonable rates. What do you think of the chairs?"

"Can you sit in them?"

Carefully, Pavo Soberano lowered himself into one of his office's five metal and imitation canvas chairs. The chair groaned and swayed. "See? They hold me, so you shouldn't have any trouble."

Jake sat. "No desk?"

"Oldfashioned, according to our decorator."

"Tell me what you've found out about Janine Kanter," suggested Jake.

Soberano said, "I went to work right after I got your faxgram yesterday, Jake. As you found out from your police friends in Greater Los Angeles, she—"

"Gomez's friends," corrected Jake. "I don't have many buddies left among the local lawmen."

The chubby detective continued. "Janine Kanter, still using the name Jean McCrea, arrived here on a Quixote skyliner flight from Greater LA. By the time the request from Lieutenant Drexler of your local constabulary arrived at Justicia, it was too late to detain the young lady. The liner had long since landed and its passengers scattered to the four winds."

"Where'd she scatter to?"

"She took a skycab to the Hotel España on the Calle de la Princesa."

"But she never actually registered there?"

"*Sí*, exactly." He spread his hands wide and gave a sad shrug. "She vanished at that point. I still have two operatives working on it, trying to find a trace of her. Do you wish us to continue?"

"Keep at it, yeah," said Jake. "I'll try a few other angles. You tried finding her under other names? She tends to stick with first names starting in J, and M's one of her favorite initials for a last name."

The detective shrugged again. "I personally checked out Josephine Macklin, Jada Mercado and Jennifer Milligan," he said. "They all arrived in our fair city on the day in question and checked into various hotels. None of them is the elusive Janine Kanter."

"She's a good actress and can disguise herself so—"

"She can't disguise her fingerprints or ret patterns, Jake. Trust me, she's not hiding under any of those aliases."

Jake leaned back, as best he could, in his chair. "What about Janeiro Martinez?"

"The best guess is that he's holed up in the Guadarrama Mountains. But so far, that's only a guess. Martinez, as might be expected, moves around a good deal."

"Okay, keep working on locating him, too."

Soberano said, "From what we've been able to find out, Jake, the Devlin Guns were delivered to Martinez. But we don't have any idea yet where they were taken."

"From what I've dug up on this guy, Martinez is supposed to be a champion of democracy. He and his bunch are opposed to President Garcia because his administration is too harsh and restrictive."

"So Martinez claims."

"But teaming up with a Teklord like Carlos Zabicas doesn't sound like something a liberal fighter for freedom would do."

"Politics often requires compromises," reminded the detective. "Martinez will take help from just about anybody."

"And why is the Office of Clandestine Operations tied in? Usually they tend to support conservative and dictatorial fellows just like Garcia."

"It's probable that your OCO has reasons for wanting Zabicas to be able to run his Tek cartel with less government interference," said Soberano. "Our *presidente* has been getting very tough on the Tek trade of late."

Jake extracted himself from the chair. The chair fell over. Righting it, he said, "We're staying at the Hotel Condor." He moved toward the door. "Let me know soon as you get anything more."

33

The uniformed police officer looked from the permit in his hand to the wall clock inside his small, narrow kiosk. "How long do you plan to be in Recinto #3, Señor Gomez?"

The detective was standing just outside the checkpoint kiosk. He had the collar of his jacket turned up, but the twilight drizzle was managing to hit at his neck anyway. "Maybe an hour."

"You're a friend of Colonel Maresca?"

"Nope, the permit to get into this section of Madrid was obtained by an associate."

The guard glanced again at the clock before returning the pass to Gomez. "There are a great many disreputable people living in the *recintos*," he said. "It's wise not to remain too long among them. You know how the poor can be."

"Spent part of my youth being poor." Gomez turned away. "And I was noticeably disreputable myself."

There was a high plastiglass wall rising up a few yards from the brightlit kiosk.

When Gomez reached the small gate in the high wall, a voxbox advised, "Pass through quickly, *por favor*. The entry will only be open fifteen seconds."

The gate snapped open, Gomez dived through the opening, the gate snapped shut.

"Show your permit to the scanner eye to return," said the voxbox.

There was a deadman sprawled in the middle of the street, facedown, and arms and legs spread wide. Two small boys, raggedy and shoeless, were crouched over the corpse going through the tattered pockets. A third boy was jabbing a metal stave at a scruffy black dog who was trying to get at the body.

Most of the buildings on this side of the wall were tumbled down and gutted. The light showing at the jagged windows came mostly from flickering candles or litelanterns. The misty air was thick with the mingled odors of cooking meat, stagnant water, urine, neowood smoke, sharp spices, damp and rot.

The boy with the stave slipped, fell to one bare knee. The wild dog, snarling, came leaping at him.

Gomez yanked out his stungun and fired.

The dog yelped once, stiffened in midair, dropped, splashing water when it hit the rutted street.

"*Gracias, tonto*," said the boy, pushing upright and kicking at the stunned dog.

"Why are you calling me stupid, lad?"

"Stupid to show an expensive gun like that around here. Somebody's going to hop you and swipe it."

Slipping the gun away, Gomez gave a negative shake of his head. "That wouldn't be a wise thing for anyone to attempt. *Adiós.*"

"*Muy tonto,*" observed the boy.

In a shadowy doorway on his left a frail teenage girl sat huddled. She was wearing a battered Tek headset and there was a crooked smile on her cracked lips.

"You have something we want, *cabrón.*"

Planted on the sidewalk a few yards ahead of Gomez was a large, broad young man in the remnants of a plaid overcoat. An electroknife rested in his left hand, whirring loudly.

"We?"

Someone coughed in the alley next to the lout in the overcoat. "My *amigos* and me."

Gomez narrowed one eye, glanced up at the rainy darkening sky overhead and then back at the lout. "What you want to do, *cachorrito*, is pretend you never tried to stop my progress," he advised. "Slink back into the alley and forget the whole incident. Otherwise, come *mañana* you'll—" Gomez's stungun was suddenly in his hand and firing.

The beam hit the large youth square in the chest. He

roared, took one thumping step ahead before dropping down onto his knees and falling face forward onto the dirty wet paving.

Gomez spun around, fired again. "Not light-footed enough," he mentioned to the thin hairless youth who'd been sneaking up on him armed with a neowood club.

While that assailant was falling toward a wide scummy puddle, Gomez sprinted out to the middle of the street.

Gun in his hand, watchful, he continued on his way. He watched the alley as he passed it.

There was another dry cough, but no one emerged to confront him.

Gomez moved on toward his destination.

JAKE'S SKYCAB LANDED in the darkening twilight. A light, misty rain was falling straight down through the increasing dusk.

"There is the house you want, *señor*," announced the robot cabbie. "The one with the spires."

"Impressive." Jake eased free of the cab.

He was on the outskirts of Madrid, and the large Victorian-style mansion covered nearly an acre of wooded land. The house had been enhanced with holographic projections, and you could see the rain falling down through the spires and turrets to hit on the core of the mansion below. Two of the projected stained-glass windows were on the fritz and they flickered, going from bright reds, blues and greens to shades of fuzzy grey.

Jake hurried up the flagstone pathway that cut through the decorative lawn to the oaken front door.

"State your business, *por favor.*"

Standing on the lawn near the wide neowood porch was a cast-iron elk. It had been fitted with a voxbox and a vidcam.

Grinning, Jake faced the metal animal. "Jake Cardigan. I have an appointment with Mr. Mockridge."

"Which Mr. Mockridge?"

"How many do I have to choose from?"

"No levity, please."

"Denis Mockridge."

"Yes, you're expected, Señor Harrigan."

"Cardigan."

"Go on inside and wait in the parlor."

Jake climbed the thirteen steps to the front door. Creaking, the door swung open inward.

There was a long shadowy hallway beyond the doorway. And to his right a dimlit room that looked to be the parlor.

Jake went into the parlor. It was furnished in the style of the nineteenth century, with fat armchairs, two bentwood rockers, heavy clawfoot tables, landscape paintings of rustic scenes, vases filled with dried flowers.

From somewhere on another floor of the mansion began the sound of a harmonium being played. A deep voice started singing, "By and by, I'm going to see the king . . ."

"I'm afraid, Cardigan, old chap, that you're hearing my brother." A small, lean man with silky white hair was standing just inside the parlor. "He's become, don't you know, something of a religious fanatic."

"You're Denis Mockridge?"

"Righto. Forgive me for not introducing myself sooner, old man." Mockridge came further into the parlor, holding out his hand. "So you're a chum of dear little Jimmy Bristol, eh what?"

"She suggested I talk with you." Jake shook hands with Mockridge.

"By and by I'm going to see the king . . ."

The white-haired man nodded at the door and it slid shut. "You must be aware of how younger brothers can sometimes be. Do sit down, old chap."

"You British?"

"Not at all, my boy. It's an affectation. Too strong, do you think?"

"Somewhat, yeah." Jake settled into one of the armchairs.

Smiling, Mockridge sat opposite him in one of the rockers. "That's the trouble with camouflage, don't you know; one tends to spread it on too thick at times."

"About the money."

"I happen to be, as dear Jimmy informed you, the largest dealer in antique American paper currency in Spain—in all of Europe for that matter."

"Has anybody offered you a large quantity of late?"

Mockridge rocked back and forth once. "What say I save us a lot of bother, old man, and state at the offset that I believe I purchased the lot of twentieth-century United States currency you're interested in two days ago in this very parlor," he said. "Jimmy and I are real chums—talknet chums. We share financial insights of one sort and another and I respect her greatly. She assures me you're a chap worth helping out."

From an inner pocket Jake took a simulated photo of Janine Kanter. "She the one?"

The rocking chair creaked when the money dealer leaned to take the picture. He brought it up close to his eyes, then moved it out to arm's length. "She had short-cropped silver hair during our negotiations; otherwise, old chap, it's the same lass."

"What name was she using?"

"Jillian Kearny."

"Do you still have the currency here?"

Mockridge shook his head. "No, it's already been split up and sold to several of my customers. I tend to move very swiftly in matters of this sort."

Jake asked, "Can you give me a rough idea of what you paid her and in what form?"

Mockridge steepled his fingers under his chin, gazing beyond Jake toward a stained-glass window that had begun to flicker. "The collection the young woman offered me is worth about three million dollars in American money," he answered. "I was able to realize considerably more than that in selling it, which is a knack I have. The young woman took somewhat less than the true value. It was paid in cash chits, drawn on a New York bank."

"Where was she staying?"

Mockridge shook his head. "She contacted me originally from Greater Los Angeles, three weeks ago, and mentioned—"

"Three weeks? That was long before—"

"Before the unfortunate Mr. Barragray met his end."

"You knew it was his collection."

"I was one of the dealers who helped him put the collection together."

Jake frowned. "Then she must have known he was going to be killed."

"Not necessarily, old chap," said Mockridge. "She called me initially to inquire if I'd be willing to purchase the collection on short notice. Well, since I do most of my transactions on short notice, I assured the lass that I would be. It was my impression that she expected the money eventually to be hers."

"Barragray was going to give it to her?"

"She was giong to come into possession in some way or other," Mockridge replied. "I often don't probe too deeply into these things, old man."

Jake asked, "Where was she staying in Madrid?"

"I don't know that. She called me and we set up an appointment for an hour later."

"Any idea where she is?"

"None whatsoever."

Jake left the chair. "I imagine you have a tap-proof phone."

"Several, old chap." He gestured toward a heavy real-wood cabinet in the corner. "You'll find one in there."

"I'd like to call Jimmy," said Jake. "I need one more favor from her."

Mockridge stood and moved to the doorway. "Give her my heartfelt best wishes, old boy."

The door opened and he stepped out into the hall.

"By and by, I'm going to see the king . . ."

34

Gomez, almost to his destination, was passing the ruins of a cafe when his trouser pocket made a small chirping sound. He stepped under what was left of a metal awning, grabbed out his palmphone. "What?"

A pack of skinny cats was fighting over something that had died in the tumble-down remains of the cafe, yowling and sputtering.

"So attending a cat fight was more important than keeping your appointment. I hestitate to call it a date, since that would connote some pleasant social aspect to what is actually—"

"*Cara*," said Gomez to the tiny image of Natalie Dent that was eyeing him reproachfully from the phonescreen,

"I've been delayed in the line of duty. I'm going to be a trifle late for our meeting."

"Trifle late? Is an hour and fifteen minutes your notion of a trifle?"

"Nat, this is not an ideal location for a spat," cut in the detective. "However, you have my word that I'll seek you out at your posh hostelry as soon as—"

"You'll seek in vain, Gomez," the Newz reporter told him. "I'm moving on in less than an hour. Which is, if you stop and reflect on the matter in that peanut brain of yours, ironic in that you stood me up and now I'm, more or less, doing the same to you."

"Where are you heading in such a rush, *chiquita?*"

Natalie frowned. "I've been getting the feeling that you're not sharing information with me anymore. So I see no reason to continue cooperating with you."

"Soon as I dig up anything, Natalie, I'll send it along to you, no matter where you are," he vowed. "Right at the moment I'm en route to see a lady known as Sister Feliz, who does good works among the poor and also manages to be a nifty source of information on the Spanish underworld. Where can I send the insights I'm going to gain?"

After a few seconds Natalie replied, "I'm heading for Santa Francesca, it's a resort town in the mountains about forty miles from here."

"Is Janeiro Martinez there?"

The rain was finding its way through the holes in the awning and hitting at him.

Natalie said, "If your investigations take you to that region, Gomez, look me up at the Encantadora Inn." She gave him a smile of a very short duration and was gone from the screen.

Gomez pocketed the phone. The cats had ceased their contest and grown silent. In fact, a stillness seemed to have spread all across the rainy side street he was on. Slowly, he resumed walking.

Then from behind him he heard the sound of running.

He pivoted around, reaching for his stungun.

There was a slim girl of fifteen coming toward him along the narrow rutted sidewalk, clad in faded trousers and a ragged pullover, her long dark hair tied back with a circle of silvery wire.

"Hurry, get off the street, *señor*," she warned, breathing hard, as she neared him.

"Any particular reason?"

She caught his arm, urging him to run. "Another raid. Los Cazadores are here."

"*Cazadores*—hunters?" He started to jog beside the darkhaired girl. "What are they hunting?"

"Us," she answered.

THREE OF THE stone walls of the small church still stood and one of them held part of a large stained-glass window showing the Annunciation. The altar had long ago collapsed, but a large crucifix still hung from a wall and the night was drenching the figure of Christ.

"Down this way." The girl, a wheeze sounding in her narrow chest, was pulling him along the side aisle of the ruined church.

Rats, disturbed by their advent, went scurrying away, skittering over the rubble and under the rotting pews.

"Explain in more detail why we're running, *cara*."

"It's a Cazadores raid. Haven't you ever heard of them?"

"I'm a *turista*."

They reached the doorway in the wall and she urged him to follow her down a shadowy stone staircase. "The Hunters haven't raided this *recinto* for nearly a month. It was overdue."

"Who are these hunters?"

The girl slipped a small literod from beneath her pullover, clicked it on and illuminated the twisted stone staircase they were descending. "They come from outside the *recintos*," she explained. "They believe, as do many in Madrid, that there are too many poor people."

"But this isn't a charitable organization, huh?"

"They have a simple solution for poverty, *señor*. They thin out the number of poor people."

"*Deus*—by killing them?"

They were deep below the ground now in what had once been a large crypt. The smell of damp earth, ancient dust and animal droppings was strong all around.

"*Sí*, killing us is their sport."

There were several stone coffins down here. They'd long since been broken into, and yellowed bones and tatters of shrouds and vestments were strewn on the cracked stone floor.

Huddling in a corner, touched now by the thin beam of the girl's literod, were three ragged children. A jawless skull lay at their feet.

"*Pobrecitos,*" the girl said to the children. "You should be safe here." She crossed to a long stone slab that had once held a coffin and seated herself atop it, inviting Gomez to join her with a gesture of her free hand.

He perched beside her, noting that he was sitting atop a memorial to an eighteenth-century bishop. "*Chiquita,* doesn't the government do anything to stop these huntsmen?"

She laughed, the wheeze rattling in her chest. "It's no secret that they encourage them," she told him. "We think they would like to see us all dead and gone. Oh, President Garcia made a speech denouncing Los Cazadores last month. Our mayor appointed a committee to look into the appalling outbreak of lawless slaughter. What will result? *Nada,* not a damned thing."

She clicked off the light and a thick, musty darkness closed in on them.

One of the children made a sad, whimpering sound.

"How many of these bastards," asked Gomez, "come over here on a raid?"

"It varies, but never less than fifty men and women. More often over a hundred."

"Nobody fights back?"

"A few try, but it's smarter to hide," she answered. "They use lazguns, needleguns—some weapons I've never heard of before. They travel in armored skycars, land them in plazas and squares and disembark. Then they travel on foot through our streets, hunting us."

"How many people do they kill in an evening?"

"Oh, usually at least seventy five or more. The children are the easiest to catch and we lose more of them. And the old people."

Gomez asked, "How long does a raid last?"

"Two, maybe three hours. Depends on their mood— and if they've been drinking a lot. When they drink, they stay longer and . . . do worse things."

He said, "Some of them were heading this way?"

"Yes, a group of a dozen or more of them set down in a square only a few blocks from where I met you."

"You've hidden down here before?"

"*Sí*, and it's always been safe." In the blackness she touched his arm. "But tonight, I'm not sure."

"Why?"

"I think they have, this hunting party, tracking dogs with them," she said quietly. "A pack of those, you know, robot hounds."

"Yeah, I'm familiar with that type of *perro*. Only recently—"

"*Quidado!*" she whispered, gripping his arm. "There's someone upstairs in the church."

The sound of heavy footfalls came drifting down into the crypt.

35

Straddling a carved wooden chair, Jake was facing the tap-proof vidphone that rested atop the desk in the living room of the Hotel Condor suite. "It might be," he said, "so long as it doesn't put you or Molly in danger, Dan."

From the phonescreen his son said, "It may not lead anywhere. But since Rex came up with the information that there might be something odd about the reports of Devlin's death—or that the guy might not even be dead— Well, I thought we ought to look into it."

"Go ahead, but be careful," his father cautioned. "We're still not sure of all the factions involved in this gunrunning mess."

"I can tell you somebody else who's connected."

"Who?"

"That operative of Bev Kendricks's that you tangled with. Jabb Marx."

"How'd you find that out?"

"Bev just phoned to ask how to contact you over there," said his son. "She's going to be calling you, but she gave me the basic facts."

"Pass 'em along now."

"Have you ever heard of an OCO agent named Gardner Munsey?"

"Munsey, yeah. He's known as the pricks' prick," answered Jake. "Marx is working for him?"

"That's what Bev thinks. Jabb was planted in her office to keep Munsey filled in on her work on the Flanders murder," said Dan. "And also to incapacitate you if he got a chance."

Jake grinned. "He let Munsey down on that chore."

"Oh, and Bev is pretty sure Munsey is either over there in Spain or on his way."

"Maybe we'll run into each other and exchange pleasantries."

"I also—"

In the righthand corner of the phonescreen a tiny dot of red light appeared and started blinking.

"Another call coming in, Dan," said Jake. "Could be Bev. I'll talk to you later."

"Okay, Dad. Bye. Molly sends her best."

Dan's image was replaced by that of Jimmy Bristol. "Me again," she said.

"You have something already?"

"Sure. I'm not calling you for another of your pious pep talks."

"No need for that anyway; one pep talk from me'll last you months," he assured her. "What about the money Janine Kanter got from your old chum Mockridge?"

She smiled. "Is he still using that awful British accent?"

"He is."

Jimmy shifted slightly in her wheelchair. "Do you want to view all the charts and graphics—or can I just verbally fill you in on what I've found out?"

"Talk to me, Jimmy."

"Okay—Janine Kanter, using the name Jessica Colburn, deposited a million, eight hundred thousand in the First Bahaman Fidelity Organization yesterday morning."

"Not in person?"

"Nope, from a trace-proof computer in the town of Santa Francesca, Spain."

"You can trace a trace-proof transaction?"

"Easy." Jimmy smiled. "Jessica Colburn is listed in the bank's nonaccessible files as the Executive Secretary of the Worldwide Pacifism Foundation. A good name for weapons smugglers, huh?"

Jake asked, "How much was in the account before her deposit?"

"Twenty-five thousand."

"That's not much."

"This gets more interesting."

"So tell me."

"Three hours—well, two hours and forty-seven minutes, to be exact—after the money was deposited, it was
withdrawn again."

"By Janine?"

"Ah, no, by a gentleman named Rafe Santos," answered Jimmy. "He's the only other person, by the way,
who can access the Worldwide account."

"Where'd the dough go next?"

"Switzerland, Zurich Fidelity. It's now in Santos's private account, along with the three million, two hundred
thousand that was already reposing there."

"Where was this Santos guy when he played with the
money?"

"Also in Santa Francesca, which isn't that far from
Madrid, you know."

Nodding, Jake said, "Any idea who he is?"

"Not so far, but I'm in the process of trying to find
out."

Resting his chin in the palm of his left hand, Jake eyed
the ceiling for a few seconds. "Wonder if Janine knows
the money isn't where she put it."

"I can't tell you that."

"I appreciate your efforts, Jimmy," he told the girl.
"Send Cosmos a bill and keep at it."

Jimmy said, "This one is on the house."

THE ROBOT DOG made a metallic snuffling sound as it came
clattering down the stone steps and into the crypt. Its

plastiglass eyes glowed an intense red, filling the musty underground room with a crimson glare.

The dog halted at the bottom of the steps, legs planted wide and silvery head low. After scanning the crypt, it started producing a loud metallic bleating sound.

"He's found some of them," shouted a woman's voice from up in the ruined church. "And none of them is armed."

She came hurrying down the stone steps. She was a heavyset woman in her late thirties, dressed in a black skirtsuit and carrying a chunky lazrifle cradled in her muscular arms. "Only *niños*," she said scornfully, frowning from the cowering darkhaired girl to the three children hunched in the corner.

The smallest kid jerked back in fright, accidentally kicking at the yellowed skull. When the skull rolled a few feet across the dusty floor, the robot dog snarled.

"Please *señora*," pleaded the fifteen-year-old girl. "We are only poor innocent children. Don't hurt us."

"What sort of prey?" called a harsh masculine voice from the top of the stairs.

"*Pequeños,*" answered the woman. "Three kids and a girl."

"You can have them all, Rosa."

Laughing, Rosa took two steps farther into the crypt. She aimed her lazrifle at the three huddled children. "The littlest first."

"Oh, please," pleaded the teen girl. "Spare them, *señora*."

Rosa swung the gun barrel around, moving closer to the girl. "I'll take care of you first, *niña*," she decided. "Then you won't annoy me while I bring down the others."

"No more sport for tonight." Gomez sat up in the stone coffin where he'd been hiding and fired his stungun twice. First at the startled Rosa and then at the snarling robot hunting dog.

Darting forward, the girl wrenched the lazgun out of the toppling Rosa's grasp.

Dust swirled upward and an ancient bone cracked when the huntress slammed into the floor.

Gomez rubbed at the disc he'd attached to his jacket, the one Silveira had given him on the island. "Still works, the hound didn't notice me at all," he said, pleased. "You all did your parts well, my children. Now, *por favor*, let's move into the next phase of the operation."

The girl hurried over and pressed her back to the wall near the entryway. She held the lazrifle against her chest. "*Señor*, oh, please," she called up the stairs. "Quickly, come and help. The *señora* has had some kind of seizure and needs your help."

After a few seconds a man called, "What are you talking about?"

"A fit, she's had a fit and has fallen to the floor. Please, I fear she's dying."

"I'm coming down," he said. "Don't try anything."

"Oh, no," she promised.

36

Thunder rumbled through the dark mountains that rose up outside the windows of Session Room #5. The lanky black man raised his hand. "I'm Leon," he said in a low nervous voice, "and I'm a Tek addict."

"Hello, Leon," said the other five people in the stonewalled room. They were seated in straightback metal chairs around a small holo stage.

Leon rubbed his left hand along his left side a few times before standing up. "I'm a little uneasy, Dr. Ortega."

Ortega was a large, wide man of fifty. He occupied the chair nearest the white bench at the edge of the platform.

"You're doing fine, Leon. This is, afterall, only your second visit to our Monasterio Tek Clinic."

The black man walked, slowly, around the platform, stopping at the bench.

A chromeplated robot came over from where he'd been standing near the windows. "Just get comfortable, Leon," he suggested in his rumbling metallic voice.

As Leon sat on the bench, lightning crackled suddenly out in the night. The black man jumped up.

The robot put a hand on his shoulder and guided him back down. "Only the storm, Leon." He attached a headset that looked like a piece of modified Tek headgear to the man's head. "Not too tight, is it?"

Reaching up, Leon tapped at the headpiece. "No, it feels fine."

"Tell him if it hurts, Leon," said a plump blonde woman from the other side of the platform.

"No, it's okay, Georgine."

The robot backed off. "All ready, doctor."

Dr. Ortega said, "You've seen the others go through this, Leon. It isn't, really, difficult."

"I know. I do want to try it." He touched the headpiece again. "The topic tonight—people that you've hurt and how you feel about it now—that's something that I still have problems with. I want to talk about my wife—my former wife."

"Concentrate on her, Leon," instructed the doctor.

"Her name is Anne."

Very dimly on the holostage appeared the image of a

slim blonde woman of thirty. When Leon looked up and saw her, he inhaled sharply.

The woman faded away.

"Relax, Leon." Dr. Ortega patted him on the shoulder. "You're doing very well. Bring her back now, concentrate on that."

Leon leaned forward, resting his palms on his knees and breathing in and out through his mouth.

Anne returned, her image sharper and clearer. Anger showed in her face and sounded in her voice. "I don't want to hear anymore of this shit from you," she said. "You keep accusing me of things I haven't done, Leon."

An image of Leon joined her on the stage, but a Leon at least ten years younger and twenty pounds heavier. "Jesus, Annie, I followed you there this time," he shouted. "I saw you with that bastard."

"Who the hell gave you the right to trail around after me?"

Dr. Ortega left his chair, patting Leon on the shoulder again. "I've just been summoned," he said, touching at his wristband. "You go right on, Leon. I'll be back very soon. You're doing fine."

The younger Leon said, "You're my wife. That gives me . . ."

Out in the stonewalled corridor Dr. Ortega hurried through the old monastery. His office was on the next level down.

When he entered, he found Gardner Munsey seated behind his desk and consulting his desk computer. "It seems," said the OCO agent, "that I arrived none too soon, doctor."

Saying nothing, the large Dr. Ortega moved around behind his desk and took hold of the lean, tanned man by the armpits. He pulled him clean out of the chair and deposited him a few feet from his desk. Taking possession of his desk chair, he said, "I don't allow anyone to use my desk in my absence, Gardner."

"That's an odd quirk," said Munsey, smiling thinly. "Perhaps some group therapy is called for."

"Why are you here?"

"I'm looking after, as always, my country's best interests, old man." Munsey seated himself in the visitor's chair.

Ortega chuckled. "Looking after Munsey's best interests." He frowned at the monitor screen. "I don't like anyone to go over my appointment schedule, Gardner."

"Come now, doctor. The fees we pay you allow me all sorts of rude and intrusive perks." He fluttered his right hand in the direction of the monitor. "You have an appointment tomorrow morning with a young woman named Natalie Dent."

"That has nothing to do with anything that you and I—"

"Ah, but it does, doctor. She's a reporter with Newz, Inc. And a very inquisitive little bitch."

"I know she's a reporter, Gardner," said Dr. Ortega, scowling at him. "She's going to interview me for that Science Celebrities segment of the nightly—"

"Natalie Dent is working on only *one* story at the moment," cut in the Office of Clandestine Operations agent. "It has to do with the whereabouts of some high-jacked Devlin Guns."

Ortega leaned back in his chair. "You're certain?"

Munsey allowed a very fleeting smile to touch his deeply tanned face. "I rarely make mistakes," he reminded. "And I certainly haven't in this instance, doctor. When the young lady calls on you, see that something nasty happens to her."

After a few seconds, the doctor nodded. "Yes, I'll have to."

WHEN THE LIGHTNING flashed, the domed living room of the mountainside villa was fleetingly illuminated. He saw her then in the intense blue glare, sitting straight and stiff in a black armchair, legs pressed together and arms folded.

From the wide arched doorway he said, "I'll turn on the lights."

"Don't, Rafe."

Darkness had taken over the room again, hiding her from him.

"Since you came back, Janine," said Rafe Santos, "you've been a pain in the ass to get along with."

"I'm always a pain in the ass, dear heart; you just never noticed before."

Lightning flashed again.

Janine was sitting exactly as she had been.

"Everything worked out in Greater Los Angeles," Santos reminded her.

"Not everything."

Santos, very carefully, came farther into the big dark living room. "Don't tell me you're mourning Dennis Barragray?"

"He wasn't supposed to be killed."

"Don't blame me. I didn't make that decision."

"Oh, I know, darling, it was an OCO decision," Janine said. "One they never bothered to tell me about."

"Barragray helped set up the gun transfer. He suggested that Peter Traynor be taken care of because he was getting too close to what was going on," said Santos, moving farther into the darkness. "He siphoned off a couple million dollars for himself and turned it into antique currency. The *hombre* wasn't what you'd call a pillar of virtue, Janine."

"They didn't have to kill him."

"Listen, all you had to do was hang around him and make sure the gun deal went through smoothly," he told her. "And once that was set up for certain, you were through with your job." He laughed. "Taking that two million in collectible currency was a bonus for us, something the OCO didn't know about. We came out ahead, and that money will help Martinez and the revolution."

"It had better."

"What do you mean?"

When the lightning came again, Janine was no longer in the armchair.

"Janine?" He whirled, trying to spot her before the blackness came back.

"Would you mind leaving me alone for a while longer, Rafe?" Her voice came from the far side of the room.

"I would mind, damn you. You sound like you're accusing me of something."

"Nothing," she said. "I'm not accusing you of a damn thing, Rafe, not yet."

"We both believe in Martinez and what he's doing. Everything I do is for that."

"What he and the Teklords are doing."

"A little more Tek on the market is better than more weeks and months of President Garcia," said Santos into the darkness. "I've been his trusted lieutenant for over three years now, working diligently for the day that is almost here. I don't like to hear you hint that—"

"I never noticed it before, Rafe dear, but there's a vid-preacher note that slips into your voice when you talk about Martinez and the cause."

Angry, he went stalking across the black room to where he figured she was. "Now *I'm* a fraud?" he slapped out with his hands, trying to locate her. "You pretend to be all kinds of different women, you sleep with anybody they order you to, and then you come and tell me that I'm the one who's a fake."

"Nobody ordered me to sleep with you."

His right hand found her and he grabbed hold of her arm. "Didn't they? How do I know it wasn't Munsey or one of those other OCO bastards who put you into my life in the first place?"

"Let go," she asked quietly.

He caught hold of her other arm and yanked her up

off the sofa she'd been sitting on. "Maybe the only one you loved was Barragray. That's why you've been so damned—"

"I never loved any of them," Janine told him evenly. "Not even you, dear heart. I'm only interested in seeing regimes like Garcia's knocked down. If that means sleeping with Barragray, then it has to be done."

He let go of her, took two steps back. Santos hadn't calculated on the coffee table and he tripped over it.

He fell to the floor, sharp pains knifing through his right side.

Janine didn't say anything.

After a moment Santos got to his feet. "In two days Garcia will be gone," he said. "Then I suppose you'll be happy."

"Then," she told him, "I'll move on to someplace else."

37

The dead wagon rolled slowly along the misty midnight street that Gomez was walking along. A large open landtruck, it had the words *Los Muertos* scrawled on its side in white glopaint.

Rattling, coughing, it halted a few yards ahead of the detective.

From the passenger side of the cab a thickset man in a heavy overcoat dropped to the rutted paving. A body, that of a thin boy of about eleven, lay facedown on the wet, cracked sidewalk. The big man made the sign of the cross, then bent and grabbed up the dead boy by the back of the shirt and the seat of the trousers.

The boy had been killed by a lazrifle blast that had cut

across his middle. When the man gathered him up, part of his insides spilled out and splashed onto the street.

Ignoring that, the man from the dead wagon carried the corpse over and tossed it into the open back of the truck. There were at least ten bodies piled there already. Climbing back into the truck cab, the man said, *"Andamos."*

The dead wagon rolled on into the night.

Gomez shook his head and resumed walking, avoiding the place on the sidewalk where the boy had been sprawled.

Less than ten minutes later he arrived at the old two-story schoolhouse that he'd been trying to reach since he entered Recinto #3.

Sıster Feliz was a small, thin woman in her middle fifties, wearing a dark sweater and trousers. "Where did she go?" she was asking Gomez.

He made a vague gesture. "I don't know—elsewhere." He'd been telling her about the girl who'd taken him to the ruined church and helped him overcome the two Cazadores who'd come hunting them. "After the raid seemed over and we left the church, I invited her to come here to your mission with me."

They were standing in a hallway just outside what had once been the school cafeteria. It was a makeshift infirmary now with twenty beds, all of them occupied, and two robot nurses in attendance.

Sister Feliz nodded. "Many people are afraid to come here."

"Isn't this a sanctuary?"

"Not completely, although the hunters and most of the gangs don't bother us."

"Soon as we saw those three kids safely home, the girl took off," continued Gomez. "She kissed me on the cheek, then went running off into the mist. I don't even know her name."

"Too bad you're not a Christian, Gomez."

"I'm a splendid fellow in spite of my heathen status."

"*Sí*, to be sure. If you had faith, though, you'd be able to accept everything that befell you tonight as God's will. Something that was meant to be exactly as it was."

Shrugging, Gomez said, "No, I'm going to keep worrying about her."

The small, thin woman told him, "I've been able to gather some of the information you wanted." Beckoning him to follow, she moved along the hall.

"How does the Lord feel about your sideline profession, Sister?"

As they moved toward the rear of the building, she answered, "He's of the opinion that the ends justify the means."

A small onetime storeroom had been converted into an office and was crowded with data-gathering equipment and gadgets.

Gomez sat on the edge of the lopsided wicker chair she motioned at. "When I checked in with my partner a little while ago," he said, "he mentioned a gent calling himself Rafe Santos. Can you dig up anything about—"

"I already know about him." She settled in front of a small desk that contained several monitors and some unorthodox attachments. "Santos is a close associate of Janeiro Martinez. Second or third in command, depending on the mood Martinez is in."

"What kind of lad is he?"

She made a sour face. "*Muy guapo,* very handsome," she answered. "Very deft at using his charm to further the cause."

"Reliable?"

"At the center, I believe, loyal only to himself. Why?"

"Would he be capable of, say, appropriating money—a lot of money—intended for Martinez and the rebels?"

"He would. Martinez, however, has a great deal more faith in him than I do." She touched a keypad. "Pay attention to the right-hand monitor. You're seeing the town of Santa Francesca."

"A very popular spot this time of year."

"Now you're looking at the Monasterio Tek Clinic. In less heathen days it was an actual monastery."

Gomez leaned forward. "This is more than a scenic tour you're giving me, I assume, Sister."

"The Devlin Guns are stored there."

"You sure?"

She smiled at him. "Nearly certain, let us say."

"Does President Garcia know what you know?"

"One or two members of his cabinet may know, but not *el presidente.*"

"Was the late Secretary of State Torres one of those who knew?"

"He knew several things that made his continued existence impossible."

"Who's behind this?"

"My sources indicate that segments of your own United States government want President Garcia gone," she replied. "And, while I don't have enough information on this yet, I'd say that your Office of Clandestine Operations has entered into some sort of deal with the Zabicas Tek Cartel. A deal that will supply continuing funds for some operation of theirs."

Gomez leaned back, his wicker chair creaked. "Did you run across anything pertaining to Janine Kanter, alias a whole mob of other women?"

"She's living with Santos at a villa in Santa Francesca."

"A versatile young lady."

"And sad."

"Oh, so?"

"She believes in the wrong things."

"That can be the trouble with faith sometimes," he said.

38

The morning sun above the mountain town of Santa Francesca filled the twisting uphill lane with brightness. The striped awnings of the white-faced buildings gleamed, the plasticobbles of the sidewalk glistened. Gomez interrupted his whistling to mutter, *"Muy triste."* Alone, hands thrust deep in his trouser pockets, he was climbing toward the Encantadora Inn to call on Natalie Dent. It was Jake's idea that his partner contact the reporter while he concentrated on tracking down Janine Kanter. "It's sad that a sensitive lad such as myself has to undertake such disheartening chores."

On the corner a child-sized silver robot was hawking faxpapers. "Read all about it," he shouted in a chirpy voice. "President Garcia's popularity climbs three percent."

"Up from what?" inquired Gomez as he passed the newsie.

"You intending to have me print you out the morning news, *señor?*"

"Nope."

"Then take a hike, schmucko."

"Exactly what I'm doing, *latita*."

The inn, narrow and made of pale grey stone, stood halfway up the next block.

Making the kind of noise people make prior to jumping off a precipice, Gomez entered the paneled lobby. He avoided the oaken registration desk and walked up the ramp leading to the second floor.

He tapped on the neowood door of Suite 213.

Nothing happened.

Gomez tapped again.

From the far end of the hall came a low chuffing noise that sounded like some ailing appliance struggling to purée rocks.

Trotting down there, Gomez found an android house dick lying on his back in a vidphone alcove. Eyes staring, legs rattling.

"*Que pase?*"

Somebody had used a stungun on the security andy. Frisking him, Gomez located a passkey.

He sprinted back to Natalie's door and used the borrowed electrokey to open it.

There was a stunned robot in there.

Sidebar, the snide robot cameraman, was spread out on his back in the center of the living room thermocarpet. The coffee table was on its side next to the bot.

"Nat?" Gomez called, drawing his stungun and crossing to the bedroom.

He booted the door open, stood back, listening.

The bedroom was empty. A bedside table had been knocked over in there and the contents of one of the reporter's suitcases was scattered across the floor.

When he returned to the living room after searching the suite, Gomez heard a sound.

Sidebar had murmured something that sounded like "putz." The robot managed to bring up his left hand and tap once at the lens of the builtin camera in his chest.

"You got pictures of something?"

Sidebar gave a positive-sounding metallic groan.

Extracting the vidcaz from the camera, Gomez crossed and thrust the caz in the slot under the vidwall.

". . . I know I don't have my symbols crossed, Dr. Ortega, and I'm certain I was supposed to meet you at the clinic and not the other—"

"Signals, Señorita Dent," corrected the large man who was facing Natalie across the living room. "The proper cliché is 'I don't have my *signals*—'"

"Be that as it may," said the life-size wall image of the redhaired reporter, "I'm darn sure I was supposed to call on you at eleven this morning. Here it is barely nine and you—"

"A change of plans has been necessitated, Señorita Dent. I won't be able to see you later and so I—"

"And who are these guys?"

Sidebar zoomed in on two broadshouldered men who'd appeared behind the doctor.

"Oh, them? *Sí*, my dear, they've come along to help carry you out the back way."

"Carry me? If you think I intend to—"

Dr. Ortega had pulled a stungun from his coat pocket and fired at the young woman.

She rose up suddenly on tiptoe, her arms flapped up and her fingers spread wide. She fell out of camera range.

"Ah, I didn't notice you standing in the bedroom doorway." The doctor fired his stungun directly at the camera.

The carpet rose up to met the falling lens and then the vidwall was blank again.

After tugging thoughtfully at his left earlobe, Gomez extracted the vidcaz and slipped it into a jacket pocket.

As he passed the fallen robot, he said, "Be of good cheer, *pobrecito*, the effects should wear off in ten or twelve hours."

Very faintly Sidebar murmured something that sounded like "putz" as Gomez hurried out of the suite.

JAKE WAS CROSSING toward the door out of his hotel room when his palmphone buzzed in his side pocket. He stopped, pulled out the phone and said, "Yeah?"

"Your phone is tap-proof, isn't it?"

Jake nodded at the image of Janine Kanter on the tiny screen in his hand. "Sure." He rested on the arm of a fat neoleather chair. "What are you calling yourself?"

"Janine will do." The slender young woman had black hair and she looked much less innocent and vulnerable than when he'd met her in Greater Los Angeles and she'd pretended to be Pete Traynor's sister. She was sitting in a highback red wicker chair in a shadowy stonewalled room.

Jake said, "I hear you're staying in Santa Francesca, Janine."

"I have to talk to you, Cardigan."

"Where?" he asked, watching the image on the small screen.

"I've found out some facts that have upset me," she told him. "I'm at a winery on the edge of town on the Calle Esperanza. It's called Los Hermanos Viñeos, Ltd. I'll be at Bodega #3, that's one of three small warehouses."

"When?"

"As soon as you can."

"I have a stop to make first," he said to the image of Janine. "I can be there in about an hour."

"That should be all right, Cardigan, but try to make it sooner."

"If it's too dangerous for you there, try to get over here to—"

"No, I'll be okay here for a while," she cut in. "Oh, and be careful coming onto the grounds. They're running wine tastings here all day and you don't want to get tangled up in that crowd."

Jake grinned. "This sounds like the last time we met."

She frowned. "How so?"

"That drunk in your apartment building, the one who insisted on inviting us in for a drink," reminded Jake. "He'd been guzzling Spanish wine as I recall."

"Oh, him, yes. I'd forgotten," said Janine. "Soon as you can, Cardigan."

"Soon as I can," he promised.

Ĥ VERY SMALL bird was singing.

"Stop that," murmured Natalie.

The bird ceased its chirping.

Her arms and her legs were stiff and sore, the bones in her skull didn't feel as though they fit together properly any longer, and she felt as though she was suffering from more toothaches than she had teeth.

Inhaling slowly, which started a series of brand-new pains all across her chest and along her ribs, Natalie opened her eyes.

The soft yellowish light of the small room jabbed into the blurry eyes. Shutting them tight, she sat up on the canvas cot she'd awakened upon. The floor was carpeted with something that felt thick and coarse under her bare feet.

"Bare feet?"

Slowly, carefully, she risked opening her eyes again. Someone had taken off all her clothes, down to her underwear, and dressed her in a stained and wrinkled blue hospital gown that was at least a half-dozen sizes too large.

Besides her and the uncomfortable cot, there was

nothing else in the room except a small goldplated bird-cage that sat on the floor in the far corner. The canary was lying on the bottom of the cage, amid a spill of red and black feed—dead.

Shivering, Natalie rested her forehead against the palm of her hand. "Dr. Ortega used a stungun on me, the so-and-so," she said to herself, remembering. "Then had those two lunks carry me here—and undress me, too, probably."

She was most likely, she concluded, at the Monasterio Tek Clinic.

"What does the doctor have in mind for me?" she wondered. "Are they going to kill me or simply keep me out of the way for a while? The coup against President Garcia is set to begin very soon and they may just want to keep me out of action until . . ."

Very slowly, the door to her room was swinging open inward.

"Don't yelp with delight, *chiquita*, or do anything else to attract attention. I've fritzed the secsystem in this wing of the clinic, but that won't last forever." Smiling, Gomez slipped into the room and shut the door behind him. "What happened to your canary?"

"He died, and before you criticize me for not spending more time on mourning the thing, tell me how we're going to get out of here." She stood up, then swayed, grabbed at the air as she fell back to the cot.

Gomez came running to her, taking hold of her arm. "Easy at first, *bonita*," he cautioned, helping her to sit upright. "They used a stungun on you."

"Dr. Ortega did it," she said quietly. "Did you say this was the Tek clinic?"

"*Sí*, you're in the bowels of the Monasterio setup." He seated himself close beside her, put a supportive arm around her. "I'm glad I found you, Nat." He lowered his arm, then slipped his hand inside the opening at the back of the gown. I've never told you this before, *cara*, but my flippant exterior masks a real affection for you."

"That's flattering, Gomez, but oughtn't we be getting the heck out of here?"

"The coast won't be clear for a few minutes." He moved his rough hand along the flesh over her ribs and then touched her right breast. "While we're waiting, Nat, we can make up for lost time."

She caught his wrist through the thin fabric of the hospital gown, tugging at it. "Don't think I'm not grateful over your risking life and limb to bust into this hellhole to rescue me, Gomez, and, as a matter of fact, if I were completely and totally truthful, I'd have to admit that you're very attractive to me even though your flaws and negative aspects would use up several bytes of—"

"Any port in a storm." Gomez took hold of her breast.

"Please, no, stop."

"This is very discouraging."

"Backsliding on her very first day with us."

"How'd she smuggle the stuff in here, Nurse 27A?"

"I have no idea, Dr. Sinjon."

Opening her eyes, Natalie discovered she was lying flat out on the cot again. "Where's Gomez?"

A lanky black man in a white jacket was leaning over

her, pulling at the Tek headset she was wearing. It became tangled in her red hair. "You're here to cure your
serious Tek addiciton, Patient Dent." Pulling harder, he
got the Tek gear free of her head, along with several red
hairs. "Who smuggled this in to you?"

"She must have a confederate in the clinic," suggested
the white medibot beside him.

Natalie glanced around the room, feeling dizzy and
hollow. "Gomez wasn't here at all, neither was the
darned canary," she said. "That was only a Tek fantasy,
induced by your hooking me up to that Tek set."

Dr. Sinjon shook the Tek gear in her face. "You're
never going to be cured if you won't accept responsibility
for your—"

"Listen, I'm a reporter, a highly respected one, with
Newz, Inc.," she told him, angry. "Soon as they hear you
louts have abducted me, they'll raise—"

"Don't you remember, Patient Dent?" asked the doctor, shaking his head sadly. "It was Newz, Inc., that had
you committed here."

39

Gardner Munsey rested the tanned fingers of his right hand against the oneway plastiglass window, tilting his head very slightly to the left. "Fairly convincing," he said, looking into the small stonewalled room at the figure in the highback red wicker chair.

"She already fooled Cardigan, even before I polished her," said the plump greyhaired woman who was sitting at the nearby image console.

"This time she's got to look convincing up close, Irma," said Munsey. "This isn't a simple phone call."

"Once the son of a bitch steps into the room," reminded Irma Bomgarner, "we've got him. It won't matter if he tumbles that she's only a holo projection and not the true and authentic Janine Kanter."

"He may have as much as five seconds to back off and get the hell out of there before the door shuts completely and he's secured."

Irma touched a keypad.

Out in the other room the image of Janine turned to smile at Munsey. She waved at him. "You're much too critical, Gardy," she said in Janine's voice. "Cardigan is going to walk right into this."

Turning his back to the observation window, the OCO agent said, "I've found, Irma, that overconfidence never pays off."

She laughed, resting back in her chromeplated chair. "I'm an expert at creating holographic images like this one," she reminded him. "The best on the damned OCO payroll, in fact. The image he saw on the phone was flawless, and this one is even better since I slicked it up. Besides, you know he's already on his way here."

"All I know for certain is that Jake Cardigan left his hotel approximately one half hour ago."

"Don't you have someone tailing him?"

"He shook the tail."

She raised her shaggy grey eyebrows. "Haven't they picked him up with aura-tracking gear?"

"He's using something that allows him to elude all our tracking hardware, Irma."

She laughed again. "Right now, then, my part of this operation is going a hell of a lot better than yours."

Munsey returned to the window.

Out in the red chair the image of Janine leaned back and crossed her slim legs. Smiling, she raised a hand in the air and gave him the finger.

"TASTE THIS," URGED the short, chubby man.

Very reluctantly, Gomez forked a small chunk of the brownish stuff into his mouth and started chewing.

"What's it taste like to you?"

After swallowing twice and blinking, Gomez answered, "Old fish, soybeans and—is it glue?"

"No, you're paying attention to the basic ingredients. You should be tasting London Broil."

"London Broil, *Padre*, doesn't have glue as one of its ingredients."

Father Romero shook his head. "That's the SinVita, Señor Gomez," he explained. "The wonderful vitamin supplement that we add to all our Comidas, Inc., meals."

"Don't your customers notice it, too?"

"You apparently have an exceptional and abnormal sense of taste."

"It smells like old fish, too," put in Gomez. "Now then, Father Romero, can we move on to—"

"Of course, of course, *sí*. There's no earthly reason why you should want to share in my joy of discovery," the blackclad priest said, sounding somewhat disappointed. "The fact that we've been able to come up with a completely believable London Broil that is totally synthetic is a cause of great satisfaction to us." He picked up a slice of imitation beef between thumb and forefinger and took a bite. "Mmm, delicious. That's London Broil, for a fact."

They were standing in a vast white kitchen next to one of the several long white worktables. The synthetic meal, in a white plate, sat on a white tray.

Gomez swallowed again, noticing that his eyes were starting to water. "Sister Feliz suggested that you could tell me about certain activities at the Monasterio Tek Clinic."

"I know a good deal about what's going on up there," replied the portly priest. "We used to own the monastery, back in the days when we were still in the liqueur business." He gestured at the dozen white stoves and the dozen or more white-enameled chefbots at work all around them. "That was before we got into the more lucrative business of mock food manufacture and catering."

"My partner and I came to Santa Francesca on the trail of a shipment of illegal weapons," Gomez told him. "Now, though, it looks like a friend of mine's been kidnapped and taken there."

"You can forget trying the local law for help," said Romero. "They have been persuaded to look the other way when it comes to the activities at the clinic."

"I figured that was the case. So what I need from you is some tips on how to get inside the damn place unobtrusively to—"

"You'd look all right in black."

"Possibly. So?"

"The Tek Clinic is one of our biggest catering customers. We deliver two hundred nourishing meals there every day, *señor.*"

Gomez brightened. "I could go in as one of your priests when the next delivery is made?"

Taking a step back, the priest scrutinized Gomez. "You don't look like the sort of fellow who'd profane the cloth," he decided. "I'm not at all pleased with what's been going on at that place of late. Is it possible, however, that in extricating your friend and locating these illicit weapons of destruction, you can refrain from putting the clinic totally out of business? Two hundred meals a day is—"

"I'll make every effort to leave the monastery standing when I'm finished," he promised. "Do you know for certain that the weapons are there?"

"I am nearly certain, Señor Gomez." He indicated the plate of mock food. "Want another bite?"

"Not at this time, *gracias.*"

"Then I'll take you into our Data Room. I actually have floor plans of the entire monastery printed on real paper," said the priest. "Plus, of course, all the most recent modifications stored in our computer."

"That would be most helpful."

After pausing to pick up another piece of imitation London Broil, Father Romero led the detective out of the mammoth kitchen.

PACING THE OBSERVATION room, Munsey said, "That's a surprising vice, Irma."

"It isn't a vice, Gardner, merely a mild bad habit." She was sitting at the console smoking a cigarette.

"Tobacco is illegal, has been for—"

"It's nowhere near as bad as Tek."

"True, but that doesn't mean—"

Out in the other room the holo projection of Janine Kanter had cried out.

Turning to face the oneway window, the OCO agent saw the figure rise up off the red chair.

Janine brought one hand to her breast, slumped and started to pitch forward. She vanished before she reached the floor.

All the lights in her room died.

"Damn." Irma was struggling with the keypad and the other controls.

"What's wrong?"

"Some kind of power outage, I'd guess."

From another part of the winery warehouse alarms started bleating.

The aircirc system was commencing to produce shuddering, rasping noises. Thin yellowish smoke started seeping into the room.

Irma pushed back and jumped free of the chair. "Some sort of massive breakdown is happening." She went trotting toward the doorway. "We've got to get the hell outside."

Munsey coughed, kept coughing. The whole room was taking on a yellowish tinge.

"This goddamn door." The heavyset woman was

pushing at the neowood door while trying to twist the handle. "Stuck."

Munsey hit the door with his shoulder, pushing hard. "Keep trying."

All at once the door went flapping open.

Irma stumbled out into the corridor, which was filling with yellow smoke and the sound of running feet.

Munsey coughing again, started running. The nearest exist to the outside was several hundred yards from here.

As he passed the open doorway of an office, someone reached out and caught hold of his arm.

Munsey was yanked into the office and the door was shut.

"Gardner Munsey, huh?" said Cardigan, poking him with his stungun barrel. "I'd like to have a chat with you."

40

Munsey said, "Apparently you didn't find the bait credible." He was sitting in the chair Jake had shoved him into.

From outside in the corridor you could still hear people hurrying out of the warehouse.

"A simulated holo never quite convinces me," he said. "I spotted that image of Janine as fake. I double-checked by asking her about something that never happened."

"The drunk with the Spanish wine?"

Jake nodded. "But I dropped in to find out who wanted to lure me here and why."

"How'd you break in here unnoticed and do all this damage?"

"It's a knack I picked up, initially while I was a cop in Greater LA," he answered. "I've only got a few minutes to talk to you, so let's cut the—"

"Interfering with a United States government agent in—"

"I imagine that officially the OCO would never admit that you're even in Spain," cut in Jake. "Fact is, it's possible that your splinter group within the agency is acting on its own. There won't be any official repercussions."

"Even so, old man, it wouldn't be smart to treat me badly."

"Oh, so? What'll you do—use a holo projection to lure me into a trap?" Jake took a small circle of blackish metal from his jacket pocket. "You know what this is. Outlawed in all civilized countries, but handy. It's a truthdisc. Once I attach it to you. Munsey, it sinks four little needles into you. You get a dose of some very powerful truth drugs and, equally important, you are hooked up to receive some very painful jolts if you fight against the drugs and don't tell the complete and absolute truth."

Munsey's tan face grew pale. "No, don't try that on me, Cardigan," he pleaded. "Please."

"Okay, then tell me where the Devlin Guns are stashed."

"I can't do that."

Keeping his stungun aimed at the agent, Jake leaned closer. "I have to know about those guns."

"You don't understand." Munsey's voice rose in pitch and he began to perspire. "Listen, I've got a skull implant that will react to the truthdisc." His left hand, which was shaking, reached up to tap at his temple. "The OCO makes sure that none of its agents will ever give away secrets. Please, don't use that. Once those damn needles break my skin—Jesus, it'll trigger the implant and I'll die within sixty seconds. You can't do it, Cardigan."

"Death before dishonor, huh?"

"Exactly, yes. You know how the OCO operates. They don't care if—"

"Let's hope you're lying." Jake slapped the disc against Munsey's tanned neck.

THE BLONDE NURSE inquired, "What did you say this stuff was, Father?"

"London Broil, my child," Gomez informed the tall, thin woman.

She tried another bite. "Has a fishy taste, don't you think?"

"I never sample our wonderful Comidas, Inc., meals." He was sharing the small office just off the clinic's large kitchen with her while two real priests carted in the two hundred meal containers. "I took a vow to eat only fresh vegetables and drink spring water."

"It hasn't done much for you." The nurse pushed aside the meal she'd chosen to sample. "I still think London Broil shouldn't be fishy."

"Well, London is a seaport afterall." Smiling beatifically, Gomez took a few backward steps. "If you'll excuse me, my dear, I must return to oversee the unloading of the rest of our healthful, nourishing meals for your poor unfortunate patients."

"You're new."

"New to you, but a longtime defender of the faith," he said. "I was only recently transferred to Santa Francesca from a quaint little church in Majorca."

Nodding, the nurse said, "The Tamale Pie last night tasted fishy, too, now that I think of it."

"I shall speak to Father Romero, God bless his loving heart, as soon as I return to the office." Smiling further, he hurried out of her office.

Once out of sight of the nurse, Gomez went hurrying along a side corridor. According to what he'd figured out after talking to Father Romero about the clinic, Janine was probably being held in the East Wing of the old monastery. He'd brought along a pocket-sized tracking device and once over there he ought to be able to pick up her aura. The maps he'd looked at had given him a pretty good idea of the layout of the place.

Gomez was wearing a black clerical suit, and the set of plastiglass Rosary beads in his coat jingled as he made his way rapidly along the twisting stone corridors.

The halls in the East Wing weren't as well lit, and a chill dampness hung in the air.

From the pocket that held the Rosary beads Gomez drew out the copperplated tracking device. It had become entangled with the beads and they came out with it and fell free.

Gomez knelt to retrieve them off the stone floor.

"I don't wish to interrupt you in your prayers, Father," said a deep voice close behind him. "But perhaps you'd better get up and tell me what in the bloody hell you're doing here."

Nᴀᴛᴀʟɪᴇ ᴡᴏᴋᴇ ᴜᴘ, very slowly.

She was still feeling the painful aftereffects of being stungunned this morning.

Or whenever the heck it was.

She had ceased to be anywhere near certain what time it was. What day, for that matter.

Sitting on the edge of the uncomfortable cot, bare legs dangling, she rubbed at the upper part of her left arm.

They'd shot something into her.

"That obnoxious medibot has an injection gun built into one of his fingers," she remembered. "They gave me something that . . . What? Put me to sleep, for one thing. But I'm very much afraid it also made me talk."

She placed her hands beside her thighs and gripped the edge of the cot. After a painful moment she was able to push herself to a standing position.

"Wouldn't you think by now that Newz, Inc., would know I was missing and come looking? Sidebar should have alerted them that I was abducted."

She took a few steps, feeling extremely unsteady and unsure.

But maybe they'd done something to the cambot. After they'd stungunned her. Used a disabler on him. Dragged him along to the clinic.

"Well, there's still Gomez. He did, afterall, have an appointment with me this morning, or whatever morning it was. Although he's got a history of standing me up, I'm pretty sure he would've dropped by this time because I know more about the Devlin Guns than he probably does. If he showed up at the hotel and I wasn't there, then he—Gomez!"

The door to her room had come swinging open inward and Gomez had entered. Smiling, he said, "That's not an especially fetching getup, *chiquita*. Not what's being worn for escapes this season. Where are your clothes?"

"I haven't even the vaguest notion as to . . ." Frowning, narrowing her eyes, she took a backward step. "This is worse than the last one."

"Beg pardon, *cara?*"

"Now you're a priest. What sort of perverse mind could choreograph a Tek fantasy in which you are—"

"*Momentito*, Nat." Gomez came across the room to her. "I am clad in priestly garb, it's not an illusion. It's all part of the disguise I used to get inside the walls."

"I suppose you're going to tell me you've fritzed the secsystem in this part of the clinic."

"I did do that, with the help of kindly Dr. Ortega."

"That's a new touch. Ortega wasn't in the last hallucination."

Gomez took hold of her arms. "Have they been forcing Tek on you?"

"Yes, and they're doing it again right now. Programming my hallucinations so I experience the most awful things."

"Listen to me, Nat. I got into this rascally institution by posing as one of the priests delivering tonight's catered meals."

"Well, there. There's a silly notion that could only show up in a Tek-induced fantasy or—"

"While making my way here I chanced to encounter Dr. Ortega. A perceptive gent, though morally corrupt, he recognized me as a crackerjack private eye and not a humble clergyman," continued Gomez. "Fortunately I was able to get the drop on him and thereafter persuade him to lend me a helping hand."

"Are you going to fondle me next?"

"*Ai, caramba!*" He let go of her and jumped a couple of feet away. "Was that part of your Tek dream?"

"Yes, it was awful."

"Awful," he agreed. "Pay attention, Nat. I am not a hallucination, but the one and only authentic Gomez come to spring you. We have to make haste out of this joint before the slumbering Dr. Ortega is missed or discovered where I deposited him. I can bop you on the coco and carry you out over my shoulder, but it will be lots simpler if you could trot along beside me."

"You are Gomez," she decided, scanning his face. "Yes, that nasty undertone to your voice was missing in the nightmare version, along with those age wrinkles all around your squinty eyes."

"We have to make a brief stop to locate the Devlin Guns," he said, pulling her in the direction of the door.

"Oh, I know where those are," she said as she followed him into the stone corridor.

41

Peppermint," said Gomez, sniffing.

"Spearmint actually." Shivering, the barefoot Natalie crossed the threshold of the low-ceilinged stone room. "The monks used to brew that vile liqueur of theirs down here."

The large room had big neowood vats lined up across it. On shelves along one shadowy wall hundreds of empty, pale green plastiglass flasks sat, dusty.

After carefully closing the heavy door, Gomez scanned the room. "Would that be the Devlin Guns over against the far wall, Nat?"

When the reporter nodded, the back of her hospital

gown snapped open. "I really wish we'd had time to locate my clothes." She refastened the gown.

Gomez, weaving his way among the minty vats, headed for the several dozen neowood crates stacked at the back of the room. "Been considerable activity down here of late, judging by all the footprints, smudges and drag marks in the dust of the centuries."

Each crate had *Estling Pharmaceuticals, Bridgeport USA* etched on its side. Gomez lifted the top crate off a stack and set it on the stone floor. *"Extraño,"* he observed, frowning down at the crate.

"What are you nattering about?" She came over to stand beside him.

Gomez crouched beside the crate. "It's too light," he said, tapping the side of the box. *"Chihauhua,* this one's already been opened."

Kneeling, Natalie lifted the lid off. "Darn."

"Nada."

The crate, except for a thin layer of plastraw across the bottom, was empty.

Gomez hefted down another box. "This one doesn't feel any heavier, *cara."*

Stretching, the reporter lifted down a crate on her own. She dropped it to the floor, knelt and lifted off the lid. "It's empty, too. How about yours?"

"In a similar state." Gomez put the lid back on the crate and sat on it. "We have several possibilities to consider now, Nat."

"The first one that occurs to you, cynic that you are, is

that I was misinformed," she said. "But I don't think so. My source—"

"I don't think you got a bum tip," he told her. "There was something in these crates and it probably wasn't drugs and sundries. But there's a good chance that the stuff has been here and gone, unloaded already and taken off by Martinez."

Natalie shook her head. "It was my understanding that the pickup wouldn't be made until late tomorrow some time," she said, sitting on the empty crate next to his. "I know I'm still pretty dippy from my Tek journey and the dope they shot into me—but I'm not wrong about the schedule."

"Schedules can change."

"I suppose, yes, that that's possible."

"There's also a chance that the guns have been high-jacked once again."

"By whom?"

"We have several contenders, *cara*. It could be the Office of Clandestine Operations decided to put the weapons to better use in some other clime."

Hunching her shoulders slightly, Natalie gazed up at the stacked crates. "I suppose, Gomez, being good and thorough investigators, that we ought to inspect every darn one of these boxes to make absolutely sure they are all empty."

"*Sí*, but I'm betting they—"

"Up on your feet, both of you." The lean black Dr. Sinjon was in the room, a lazgun in his right hand. "Get the hell away from those guns."

"It's Dr. Sinjon," Natalie said to the detective. "He's in cahoots with Dr. Ortega."

"Judging by the vidphoto I've seen, you must be Sidney Gomez of the Cosmos Detective Agency," said Sinjon, moving closer. "The picture flattered you."

Making his way through the vats, he stopped close to Gomez. Glancing down into the open crate, he jabbed the barrel of the lazgun into Gomez's side. "Damn you, what the hell have you done with the guns?"

"Nonsense," said Molly Fine.

"There's a lot I admire about you," Dan told her, "but your fondness for stunt flying is not one of—"

"For a callow youth who claims he's got detective blood in his veins," she said, looking away from the control panel of her lemon-yellow skycar long enough to give him a pitying smile, "you sure don't seem to be able to tell the difference between expert handling in traffic and dangerous grandstanding."

"Hey, I'm barely a year younger than you," he pointed out. "So dragging my age into what was rational discussion doesn't—"

"Truce," suggested the girl.

It was late afternoon and they were heading along the coast toward Dan's condo apartment. They were at an altitude of 5,000 in the hazy sky.

Dan grinned. "Okay, I won't mention your suicidal skydriving if you'll forget that I'm the youngest of your many suitors."

Molly said, "Matter of fact, I think I used to date a kid who was even— Damn!"

As the skycar swung sharply to the left, Dan sat up. "What's wrong?"

Molly was punching at control keys. "Don't know," she answered. "I don't have control of the car anymore."

The skycar descended a thousand feet, flew across the wide stretch of beach and then shot out over the afternoon Pacific. It continued to lose altitude.

"C'mon," Molly said to the dash. "Give me back control."

Dan jabbed at a dash button labeled *Help*.

The small screen above the button came to life and the words *Help Menu* appeared in red across the top. Below that there was only a single phrase—*You're beyond help, kiddies.*

Dʀ. Sɪɴᴊᴏɴ Sʟᴀᴘᴘᴇᴅ Natalie, hard, across the face. "Maybe you can answer me," he said angrily.

"*Cabrón.*" Gomez took a lunging step toward him.

"I don't need both of you alive," he reminded, jabbing the lazgun barrel into Gomez's side once more.

"It's okay, Gomez," said Natalie, her eyes watering as she rubbed her hand across her cheek.

Sinjon repeated, "Where are the guns?"

"Listen *tonto*," said Gomez evenly. "You ought to be able to figure out that we didn't swipe your goddamn guns."

"I find the two of you here and the guns gone. That—"

"Natalie was locked up in one of your cages until a few minutes ago," reminded the detective. "You know that."

"Maybe, but I don't know how long you've been roaming around down here, Gomez."

"*Sí*, I've been wandering around with a crew of free-lance movers. Use your *cabeza*, doc."

Scowling, he said, "It must be you."

"When's the last time you actually saw the guns?"

"Two days ago, when they arrived."

"You saw the guns, laid your very own eyes on them? Not merely the crates?"

"We opened several of the crates. There were definitely guns in the—Wait, now!" The doctor gave an angry shake of his head. "Playing detective games with you isn't going to help."

Gomez held up his forefinger and touched it. "We didn't take the guns," he said, then tapped the next finger. "You say you didn't move 'em either." He touched a third finger. "Ergo, it was somebody else. Who?"

"Martinez's people will be here tomorrow to pick up the guns. What the hell are we going to—"

"See?" Natalie nodded at Gomez. "I told you it wasn't going to be until—"

"Quiet," ordered Dr. Sinjon. "I've got to find Dr. Ortega and—"

From out in the hallway came a loud crash. It sounded as though a large robot had suddenly fallen over.

That distracted the doctor, which caused him to look toward the door.

Jumping, Gomez slammed a fist into his stomach.

Then he grabbed the wrist of his gun hand, and levered him, hard, against the side of a high neowood vat.

Sinjon gasped, made a choking noise.

Gomez twisted the man's wrist until the lazgun dropped to the dusty stone floor.

Before the doctor could straighten up, Gomez kneed him in the groin.

As Sinjon cried out in pain and doubled over, Gomez booted him twice in the chin.

Sinjon fell against the vat again as he dropped to the floor.

Gomez dived, snatched up the lazgun and moved to stand over the sprawled body. Sinjon was unconscious.

"Good lord, Gomez, you came near to killing him."

"He shouldn't have slapped you." He caught her arm, shoving her behind the vat. "Hunker down here while I see what caused the commotion outside."

He ran across the room, managed to get behind the vat nearest the doorway as the heavy door came creaking open.

Gomez remained hidden, watching the figure in the doorway. Then, nodding to himself, he stepped into the open. "What brings you here, *amigo?*"

"I had a tip the Devlin Guns were here," answered Jake, grinning. "And you?"

"Came for the guns and Natalie."

"Find them?"

"He found me." Natalie, tugging her extra-large hospital gown into place, came striding over to them. "But the guns seem to be long gone."

42

Everything's been taken over or incapacitated," said Molly. "We can't even phone out."

"Why? Who's doing this?"

The yellow skycar had been flown out several miles from the Greater LA coast. They were flying only a few feet above the pale blue Pacific.

Dan gave the door handle another try. "If I could get this open, maybe—"

"Here's something we'd like you to think about."

"Dan!"

The vidphone screen in the dash had turned itself on. A skull showed on the screen, its jaw fluttering as it spoke.

"Consider this, kids," the death's-head said. "It would be extremely easy to carry this one step further. Dive your showy skycar right into the ocean."

"Who the hell are you?" asked Dan.

"A concerned citizen." The skull laughed. "And here's the sales pitch. Quit trying to find out if Devlin is alive or dead."

The screen went black.

Molly touched the controls and her skycar started to climb. At 3,000 feet she turned it back toward land. "Jesus," she said.

"Hokum," said Dan.

"A death's-head is a mite melodramatic."

"Shit, they're treating us like kids—whoever they are."

Molly gave him a gentle nudge, then put her finger to her lips. "Well, we are kids, Dan," she said quietly, sounding uneasy. "I don't know about you, but I'm scared."

"I suppose you're right, Molly. But it ticks me off to have to give in."

"We don't have any choice, do we? They could have killed us."

Sighing, Dan said, "You're right, we'll have to quit." His voice sounded frightened and resigned, but anger and determination showed in his face.

RAFE SANTOS YELLED. He threw the palmphone to the carpeted floor of his den. "Janine!" He shouted again, running out into the hallway. "Janine, where the hell are you?"

The villa remained quiet.

"*Puta!*" he yelled.

She was in the kitchen, wearing a white shirt and dark trousers, sitting at the raw wood table with a cup of steaming herbal tea in her hand. "Looking for me, dear heart?"

He came striding across the room and slapped the cup out of her hand. "*Perra!*"

The hot tea splattered the front of her white shirt, splashed the tabletop. The cup smashed against the high white cabinet behind her. "Something's upsetting you, Rafe?"

Leaning down, he grabbed hold of her shoulders. "Where are the damned guns?" he shouted. "*No me jada,* Janine! Just tell me."

She shoved back in her chair, twisting free of his grip and standing up. "They're gone from the monastery."

"I damn well know they're gone." Standing wide-legged, he scowled at her. "Sinjon just called me. Your goddamn friend Cardigan was there at the clinic. They stungunned Dr. Ortega, dragged that Newz bitch away. But he doesn't think they took the Devlin Guns."

"That's right, they didn't."

"You took them."

She said, "I arranged to have them moved."

"Why? Have you sold out to Garcia?"

Janine smiled. "Speaking of selling out, Rafe," she

said. "I found out that you haven't been completely truthful with me."

"What's who I sleep with got to do with—"

"Not the other women, that never bothers me," she cut in. "No, it's the money, Rafe dear. The money I took from Barragray was meant to help fight against the Garcia regime."

"That's exactly what it's doing."

"Explain how that works—since it's in your private account in the wilds of Switzerland now, love."

Santos lowered his head for a few seconds, fists clenched at his sides. "We aren't all dedicated as you are, Janine," he said finally. "In case something goes wrong, in case we fail, I want to have money to—"

"And you didn't feel you were obliged to mention that you'd swiped the money?"

"If I had told you, Janine, you'd simply have had a tantrum and—"

"I see," she said, resting her right hand on the handle of the cabinet door.

Santos said, "The real point is, whatever you think of me, that Martinez needs the guns. They're an important part of the coup plan and without them—"

"I'm afraid Janeiro's going to have to improvise."

"No, we've got to have the Devlin Guns. It gives us an advantage that otherwise—"

"I'm withdrawing my support, Rafe dear," she said. "While I was finding out about what you really did with the money, I gathered some other interesting information about this whole alleged revolution I've been helping. It turns out that the OCO—or at least the extreme faction inside that outfit—hasn't been exactly truthful either."

"*Perra*, I don't have time for a lot of political theory crap. It's the whereabouts of the Devlin Guns that—"

"It seems these OCO fellows have made a deal with the Zabicas Cartel to get financing for some very dubious guerrilla movement in Brazil. I mean, Jesus, the administration in Brazil is rotten enough as it is, but these OCO darlings are even worse."

Quietly Santos told her, "I'll have to make you tell me where the guns are, Janine."

She opened the cabinet behind her, reaching inside. "You're right, Rafe. I should be more cooperative with you." Smiling, she took a snub-nosed, ivory-colored handgun off a shelf. "Okay, here's one of the guns."

"Janine!"

Pointing the Devlin Gun at him, she fired.

Santos had started to reach for the lazgun tucked into his waistband.

But the soundless, unseen touch of the gun hit him.

An odd, sad, mewing cry came spilling through his lips. From inside his body came grating, splashing noises.

He tried to make a pleading gesture toward her, but his hands and then his arms collapsed into dangling, bulging bags of skin. Fragments of bone made hundreds of punctures in the skin; blood and fluid came dribbling out.

His skull dissolved, leaving just a collapsing, puckering balloon of wrinkled flesh and hair.

The bloody, foul-smelling mess that had been Rafe Santos just a moment before went splashing to the floor, spilling blood and bile and body fluids.

Janine, lowering the gun to her side, stepped aside to avoid getting her shoes splashed by the spreading spill of liquids.

From the kitchen doorway Jake said, "Evening, Janine."

"Jake." She lifted the gun and aimed it at him. "I was hoping you'd stop by."

43

Jake was sitting on the opposite side of the villa living room in a grey armchair. "You found out about what he'd done with the money, huh?"

Shoulders back, knees together, Janine sat on the sofa with the Devlin Gun resting in her lap. "This probably sounds strange after you just saw me kill Rafe," she said, "but I'm an idealist. He betrayed what I thought was a cause that I could work for."

"It's not your cause anymore?"

"No," she said. "How'd you find your way to the Monasterio Tek Clinic?"

"Gardner Munsey confided in me, told me the guns

were stored there," answered Jake. "I used a few tricks I've acquired and got past their secsystem at the clinic." He shrugged. "The guns were no longer there and it occurred to me that you might have had something to do with that."

"I did. Where's that bastard Munsey now?"

"After our chat, I used a stungun on him," he said. "Then I left him at a spot where another US government agency could collect the guy. They're dedicated to curbing the OCO's more uncivil activities."

"That's right," she said, fingers stroking the handle of the gun, "you and Bascom are thick with all sorts of intelligence types."

"Bascom is," he corrected. "I'm just a plain and simple private investigator."

"Cynical Jake Cardigan," she said. "You kidded me in Greater LA about being a naive kid."

"I thought you were younger then. You're a convincing actor."

"Yes, that's true. It probably comes from never being quite sure who I really am."

"I'd like to find the Devlin Guns, Janine."

She watched him for a few silent seconds. "You're probably a lot more honest than most of these bastards," she said. "And, maybe, more of an idealist than I am."

Jake grinned, saying, "Naw, it's only a knack I have for giving false impressions."

She rose up, holding the Devlin Gun at her side. "I'm

going to leave here," she said. "The guns are stored here, down in what used to be a dungeon some centuries ago. I had them brought in while Rafe was off in the mountains consulting with Martinez."

"Weren't you afraid he'd find them?"

"It wouldn't have mattered," she said. "As soon as I learned about what he'd done with the money, I knew I was going to kill him."

"You don't intend to let Janeiro Martinez have the guns?"

"No, I made a mistake about him, too," she said, moving toward the doorway. "I'm trusting you to see that the Devlin Guns get to someplace where they can't be used."

"I'll do that," he promised.

"For a while I'm going to be inactive. Eventually I'll find something to work for." She held up the gun as she went out of the room. "I'm keeping this one for a souvenir."

JABB MARX'S HIGHLY chromed skycar set down in the middle of a dark grassy field that was surrounded by what looked like jungle. The safety gear unhooked and the door on his side flapped open.

"Last stop, all out," announced the dash voxbox.

"What the hell is going on?" The big wide man whapped the dash with his fist. "Why'd you land me here?"

Something roared out on his left.

It was a large lion. Head slightly lowered, the beast was loping across the grass toward him.

"Up, take me away from here," he told his skycar, punching at the controls. The car didn't respond. "Good Christ." Marx grabbed at the door handle, trying to pull it shut. The door remained stubbornly wide open.

"It's only a robot lion."

Marx jerked in his seat and gazed to his right. "How'd you get in my car?"

Bascom appeared to be sitting in the passenger seat. "It's a holoprojection, Jabb, my boy."

"Where are we?"

"Santa Monica Sector ElectroZoo. Don't you ever come here?"

"Just because you run a hotshot detective agency, Bascom, doesn't give you the goddamned right to—"

"I wanted to have a little conference with you."

The lion stopped beside the open door and began sniffing curiously at Marx's left leg.

"Go away, get the hell out of here," he told the furry mechanism. "They're built not to attack people, aren't they?"

"Sure—unless somebody's tampered with this one."

"I'm getting some nice stuff for a lawsuit against you," warned the big man. "It's illegal to take over the control of a skycar in—"

"Yeah, but the notion appealed to me so much," explained the head of the Cosmos Detective Agency. "Since you used the same gimmick on Dan Cardigan and Molly Fine only a few hours ago."

Marx raised his hand to swat the lion, then thought better of it. "I don't know any—"

"After Dan told me what had happened, I started doing some digging," the projected Bascom said. "Wasn't too difficult to trace the whole operation to you."

"You can't establish a damn—"

"Skull faces, Jabb? C'mon now, really."

"I didn't threaten those kids and I had nothing to do with sending their skycar out over the damned Pacific Ocean."

"No, my sources aren't wrong this time, Jabb," Bascom told him.

"Take a jump for yourself, Bascom."

Snarling, the lion reared up and plopped both heavy paws in Jabb's wide lap.

"Get away, go."

Bascom continued, "You were hired by some of your OCO chums to throw a scare into the kids, persuade them not to keep trying to find out if Devlin is truly dead."

"I have nothing to do with the Office of Clandestine Operations," insisted Marx. "Until that bastard Cardigan screwed me up with Bev Kendricks, I was a private—"

"I'm in the process of seeing to it that nobody in Washington bothers Dan or Molly again," cut in the image of Bascom. "But I wanted personally, or almost personally, to suggest to you that you leave them alone, too. Best course for you to follow, my boy, would be to resettle in some other state. Learn a trade and forget about being a toady for the intelligence boys."

"You can't order me to—"

"Take a couple of days to mull this over." Bascom vanished.

Across the night field came two more lions.

44

Jake waited for roughly two minutes after Janine had slipped away. Then he took out his palmphone and tapped out a number.

Gomez, surrounded by darkness, appeared on the tiny screen. "Is all well, *amigo?* I've been chilling my favorite portions while lurking out here watching the villa and covering the backside."

"It's okay, yeah. Janine is leaving here, but the guns are supposed to be stored below."

"Supposed? You allowed that multifaceted *mujer* to escape before you made certain about the weapons?"

"It wasn't a question of allowing, since she was carrying a Devlin Gun."

"Ah."

"And I decided to trust her."

"I tend to trust armed women, too."

"Contact Bascom from the skycar vidphone, Sid," suggested Jake. "Arrange for the local branch of whatever Washington agency he's in cahoots with to get here fast and gather up these damned guns. Then come on in here. I'll be down in the subbasement."

"What's the status of Santos?"

"He's gone to his reward."

"Thanks to you?"

"Nope, Janine arranged that."

"Hallelujah, I find out a new talent of hers each and every day," said Gomez. "She's an inspiration to a youth such as myself."

Jake pocketed the phone, then headed downstairs.

He located the guns where Janine had told him they'd be found, far beneath the villa in a large room that had been cut out of the mountain. The Devlin Guns were in unmarked plazcrates, six guns to a box, stacked all along one rough stone wall.

Some remnants of the days when the underground room had been a dungeon remained. There was a wooden stretching rack, a brazier for heating hot irons, a scatter of chains and manacles.

Jake lifted one of the stubby, off-white guns out of its box, hefted it in his hand and then put it back.

Behind him a boot scraped on the stone floor.

Not turning, he said, "You're getting impressively swift, Sid."

"He won't be joining you, asshole."

Almita was in the old dungeon with him.

"Where is he?"

She shrugged one shoulder. "I don't know exactly where he fell after I shot him."

"THIS IS, AND I hate to be critical of the guy after he almost literally plucked me from the maw of destruction, typical of the way Gomez can let me down in moments of need."

"Jaws," corrected Sidebar. The cambot was sitting in an armchair with his large metallic feet up on a hassock. "It's jaws of destruction."

He and Natalie were sharing an office in the Madrid offices of Newz, Inc.

"To someone who's chock-full of clichés maybe." The reporter, wearing a mint-green skirtsuit, was sitting on the edge of a Lucite desk with a talkwriter mike in her hand. "He promised to contact me here soon as he and Jake had news about the Devlin Guns."

"You should have tagged along with them."

Natalie sighed. "It's astounding how I'm surrounded by a sea of ingratitude," she mentioned. "I came back to Madrid to find out if you were okay. My concern for you, however, doesn't seem—"

"You need a good cameraman. It wasn't my well-being that—"

"And, though this may not make sense to you since they didn't build any human feelings into you, I was very anxious to shed that dreadful hospital garment those goons at the clinic had decked me out in," continued

Natalie, spreading her arms wide. "Does this outfit look all right for an important newscast, Sidebar?"

"To someone without any human instincts builtin, it looks okay." The robot leaned back, locking his hands behind his metal skull. "You also persuaded the Newz, Inc., dimwits to let you do a special vidwall broadcast tonight."

"Well, it's a heck of a big story," she reminded, smiling. "It's certain to throw a scanner in the works of Janeiro Martinez's planned revolution."

"A spanner is what people toss."

"I doubt they'll try the coup now, so Garcia, who seems to me to be the lesser of two evils, although he is a very short and unattractive man, but that doesn't much matter in politics, I suppose, will stay in power for a while," said Natalie. "And I'm betting that the Office of Clandestine Operations will be forced to clean house again. On top of which, Sidebar, the reasons for the murders of Peter Traynor and that Flanders fellow will come out in the open. Traynor's wealthy ex-wife and her two kids will be safe from—"

"The power of the press is a wonderful thing."

Pointing the mike at him, Natalie said, "I know what's gnawing at your innards. They're letting me go out and simply sit there and look the viewers right in the eye and tell them all the news I've dug up. Without any of your distracting vidfilm to get in the way. You hate to admit that I can hold millions of well-informed viewers in my spell without a single—"

"A mongoose can do the same thing with a snake."

"Exactly, and they don't need video footage either."
She tapped the talkwriter mike on her knee, then set it
aside and dropped from the desk. "Darn, I'm due to go
on worldwide in sixteen minutes. Pinpointing the location of the Devlin Guns will make such a terrific tag for
this report." She frowned at the vidphone atop the desk.
"C'mon, Gomez. Call me, darn it."

The phone remained silent.

"You're *NADA*. You didn't count for anything," Almita told
Jake. "Martinez is still going to get these Devlin Guns
and everything will go just the way Carlos Zabicas
wants."

"Not exactly," he said.

"Why not, asshole? I figured out where the guns must
be once I heard they were gone from the clinic," she said.
"I've got them now and, once I fix you for good and all,
I'll phone Carlos to send a crew to—"

"In a shade less than ten minutes there'll be a Newz,
Inc., broadcast going out." Jake took a step to his right.
"They'll outline the whole damn plan that your boss and
Martinez and the OCO worked out. That's really going
to make it difficult for you folks to do a damn thing."

"Bullshit."

"What you really ought to be doing is packing," he
suggested. "You're going to have to hide out, because
President Garcia is going to crack down even more on
the Tek cartels now."

"We've got the guns. We can still make a lot of trouble."

"Maybe, but you've sure as hell lost the element of surprise."

She shook her head from left to right twice, angrily. "No, I don't believe you."

He pointed a thumb at the low, beamed ceiling. "There's a vidwall up in the living room of the villa," he said, taking another step to the right. "Let's go up there and watch the Newz show when it comes on. After that, Almita, you'll probably decide to—"

"You're just stalling, hoping someone'll get here to save your miserable ass."

"It's your ass you ought to be worrying about."

She lowered her gun hand, eyes narrowing. "All right, *cabrón*, we'll watch TV together." She nodded at the doorway.

When Jake started to move, his feet seemed to get tangled with a spill of chain on the old dungeon floor. He stumbled, fell to one knee.

He came up clutching a length of the heavy rusty chain and swung it at the young woman.

Almita brought up her lazgun and squeezed the trigger.

The end of the chain hit her wrist and the barrel of the gun tilted up. The sizzling beam cut one of the wooden beams in two.

Jake snapped the chain again, knocking the gun from her hand. Diving, he grabbed it up from the floor.

"*Cochino!*" she said, rubbing at her wrist.

"Upstairs," he advised, gesturing with the gun.

Gomez was tiptoeing across the living room when they got up there. "Ah, I'm too late for the festivities," he complained.

Jake grinned. "Glad to see that you aren't dead," he said. "Almita was under the impression she'd knocked you off, Sid."

"The *señorita* is far from being a topnotch marksman, especially at a distance," explained his partner. "It seemed wise to dive into a handy gully and pretend to be defunct until she'd moved on. Then I headed for here."

Almita made an angry spitting noise. "I thought I'd taken care of at least one of you assholes."

"Alas, no, *angelica*," said Gomez sympathetically. "And this was the last chance you're ever going to have, too."

45

Gomez stepped out of the skyport vidphone booth, shaking his head forlornly. *"Nada,"* he reported. "Sister Feliz hasn't been able to find out a damn thing about the girl. And the op from Soberano's Maravilla detective agency hasn't found a trace of her either."

Picking up his suitcase, Jake asked, "How important is this?"

"I don't know," his partner answered. "She's just a kid who helped me when those hunter bastards were trying to turn me into a trophy. I don't know—I'm just concerned about her."

"Want to stay in Madrid and find her?"

Gomez sighed. "Nope, I guess not," he said. "This

isn't a romance thing, *amigo*. What it really is—well, I'm getting old. I feel paternal toward her and I'd like to be sure she's going to do okay."

"Soberano's likely to locate her before too long."

Bending, Gomez gathered up the bag he'd set down next to the booth. "*Sí*, and when he does, I can do something to improve her lot."

Jake reminded, "Our skyliner for Greater LA leaves in twenty minutes."

"Paternity at a distance is more in my line anyway." He started heading for their departure ramp.

Holocommercials for nearcaf, wine and botsoccer floated overhead.

"Hey, wait up, Gomez!"

He hunched his shoulders and halted. "*Ai*, it's the telltale cry of my nemesis."

Natalie, dodging around passengers and baggagebots, was hurrying toward them along the tinted plastiglass ramp. "Hello, Jake," she said when she caught up with them. "Gomez, I'm glad I found you, and I won't even take precious time, since the liner's about to depart, to criticize you for scooting out of your hotel without so much as a fare-thee-well or—"

"You're not booked on our flight, *cara?*"

"How could I be? I have to remain here in Madrid for at least two full working days to follow up on this whole business. The failed revolution, the locating of the stolen guns, the sinister links with the OCO—the whole complex mess. I'm doing a nightly broadcast and a whole slew of minireports and a summing up for Newz's week-end service." Reaching out, she put both arms around him and hugged him enthusiastically. "I really appreciate your help and particularly your taking the time, after you'd been about as close to the brim of death as you could possibly be, to vidphone me at our studios just forty seconds before airtime to confirm the location of the Devlin Guns and, honestly, I won't even mention that in the future I'd really appreciate it if you could get me information like that at least five minutes ahead of broadcast so that I can make sure it gets into my script in the polished yet breezy style that my millions of viewers—"

"*Chiquita,*" cut in Gomez as he extricated himself from her enthusiastic embrace. "We have to take our leave."

"Certainly, don't let me detain you," she said. "I simply took time out from my impossibly crowded schedule to rush down here to wish you a heartfelt bon voyage, Gomez."

"*Gracias* and *adiós.*"

She caught hold of his arm, pulling him back toward her. "Oh, and, Gomez, I've been thinking about that strange and awful Tek-induced nightmare I had, the one, as I believe I mentioned, where you expressed a deep passion for me," she said. "While you're winging your way homeward, you might want to think about that notion and, as repellant as it is to me, determine if perhaps there's a grain of truth in it. It would explain some of the odd aspects of our long-running relationship." She kissed him on the cheek and let him free.

"I'll give it my unswerving attention," he promised, taking off at a trot up the ramp.

THE AFTERNOON SKY over Greater Los Angeles was a sooty golden color. Jake, alone in his skycar, was flying inland.

On the dash phonescreen Bascom was saying, "Concentrate on the bonus. It'll be substantial for both you lads."

"The Devlin angle is a loose end."

"For now," conceded the head of the Cosmos agency. "I've already assured you that nobody is going to bother your son or Molly Fine over this."

"But is this guy alive?"

Bascom said, "Thus far I haven't been able to find out. However, Jake, it occurs to me that I may be able to persuade certain interested parties in our nation's captial to finance an investigation." He held up his hand. "That will be *another* case. This one is officially over."

"Okay."

"Oh, and I'm curious about an item that just came in from Madrid. Why am I still being billed by Soberano's agency in Madrid?"

Jake looked away from the phonescreen. "It's all part of the case."

"Says here Gomez authorized these further investigations," said Bascom. "Can I deduct these charges from his bonus?"

"It would not," advised Jake, "be a good idea, chief."

"All right, benovelent patriarch that I am, I'll forget about the matter. Unless it goes on beyond the end of the week." Bascom ended the call.

Jake tapped out a landing pattern and the skycar began drifting down toward a simulated nature preserve in the Pasadena Sector.

Bev Kendricks was waiting at the edge of the landing lot. Holographic redwood trees rose up behind her, with mossy trails winding through them. "Most of what I said to you when you got into that fight with Jabb Marx I didn't really mean," she began as he came toward her.

He put his arms around her for a moment, then stepped back. "But some of it you did believe."

"You've been hanging on to your anger over Beth's death a long time," she said.

He said, "I'm not ready to give it up yet."

She hesitated a few seconds, then took his hand. They walked into the deep shadows of the forest.